LEGACY
SOUL

HAND OF FATE BOOK TWO

LEGACY
SOUL

HAND OF FATE BOOK TWO

SHARON JOSS

AJA PUBLISHING
USA

Also by Sharon Joss

Novels:

Arum
Brothers of the Fang
Steam Dogs

(Hand of Fate Series)
Destiny Blues
Legacy Soul
Chaos Karma

Novellas:

Stars That Make Dark Heaven Light

Short Story Collections:

Dreams of Flesh and Blood (Horror)
Solace Amid the Planets (Science Fiction)

CHAPTER 1

TWENTY-SEVEN MINUTES LATE, the number eleven bus to Shore Haven roared up to the stop in front of me, in a scream of air brakes and great rolling gout of black diesel. Even without the smoky bus belch, my eyes felt like they were on fire; I'd just gotten new contact lenses, and hadn't gotten used to them yet. I muttered a silent oath and climbed aboard, my mood having already been poisoned by the unexpected and sudden demise of Trusty Rusty, my nine-year-old Honda earlier in the day. My bulky helmet banged against my leg as I made my way through the tightly-packed bus, looking for a seat, but of course at 5:45pm on a Friday afternoon in mid-August, all the seats were taken.

Pressed tightly on all sides by a sweaty mass of humanity, I gritted my teeth and held on to the overhead bar as the bus swung out into traffic again. *Five stops to go.*

I'd called my half-brother Lance for a ride and a

tow, but he wasn't answering his cell. His auto body shop services all the city vehicles, and if I didn't get Rusty out of the lot by midnight, the City of Picston would give me a ticket and impound it. Pretty ironic, since I'm a Picston parking control officer.

Three stops later, the number of people getting off far exceeded the number of people getting on, and the bus began to empty out. Gratefully, I slid into an empty seat for the three-mile ride to Shore Haven.

I smelled the *djinn* as soon as I sat down.

Djinn are unnamed *djemons*, or demons, as they're more commonly known. In the *djinn* stage, they're stinky little apparitions which are imperceptible to everyone but the person they're trying to attach themselves to.

And me.

The reek of licorice tinged with a hint of sulfur is unmistakable. Once *djinn* attach themselves to a master, are named and given their first command, the scent disappears, and they're able to materialize in the physical world as real demons. But by that time, they're yours for the rest of your life.

And I should know. I've got two baby *djemons* of my own.

I scanned the half-empty bus; looking for the source of the stink, but no dice. When the bus stopped at the corner of Third and St. Joseph's, I stepped out into the humid afternoon, only to be hailed by a woman behind me.

"Excuse me, are you Miss Blackman?" The roar of the departing bus drowned out the rest of what she said.

As soon as I spotted the demon coiled around her neck I knew what she wanted.

As she spoke, a gust of soot whipped her frizz of reddish hair into a wild halo. "I'm looking for the Hand of Fate."

CHAPTER 2

SHE SAID I could call her Jane. Jane Jones.

Yeah, right.

She was desperate for help; the demon was ruining her life. She was terrified of snakes. She was a teacher, she explained—third grade. She'd lose her teaching credential if anyone found out she had a demon. She couldn't sleep; couldn't eat. The other two demon exterminators in town had recently shut their doors, and she'd heard I could get rid of it.

Yes.

The word was getting out. A few weeks ago, someone had cracked open a cave full of *djinn* and they'd been running loose in Shore Haven, attaching themselves to unsuspecting people just like Jane.

We trudged up the sidewalk toward my apartment, the smell of hot asphalt and diesel fumes adding to the grime of my already sweat-dampened hair and clothes. All I wanted now was a shower and a beer, but banishing her little guy would only take a minute.

She followed me up the driveway of my landlord's house; a forgettable 1940's detached avocado green split-level ranch with white trim and a big oak tree in the front yard. Up a narrow driveway leading around and behind the garage to the very back of the property to where I lived in a one-bedroom apartment above a 150-year-old stone stable. As we passed the garage, I stopped dead in my tracks.

More than a dozen people clustered in the paved area in front of my apartment. The only person I recognized was Miriam, "Mimsy" Wu, the manager of the House of Cards; a restaurant and gaming establishment in Rochester, which until recently, catered to my stepbrother Lance's gambling addiction.

"What's going on?" I asked.

"It's about time you showed up. Some of us have been waiting here for hours." Chopstick-thin Mimsy wears tiny, expensive-looking clothes that I've never seen at any of the places I shop, and if those eyelashes are real, I'll eat a bug. "Where have you been?"

"My car died. I had to take the bus."

She gave me a cat-eyed smile. Probably never been on a bus in her life. Her great-grandmother and mine were best friends, so I feel like I have some sort of screwy obligation to be nice to her. On the other hand, she probably slept with my boyfriend in the not too distant past; something I haven't had a chance to do yet.

"Mimsy says you're the new Hand of Fate," a middle-aged woman in lavender seersucker capris appeared to be the self-appointed spokesperson. "Are you taking over Madame Coumlie's appointments?"

Madame Coumlie was my great-grandmother. She died a few weeks ago and her abilities and legacy as the Hand of Fate passed to me. The whole Hand of Fate concept was still a bit fuzzy for me. So far, I'd banished a whole boatload of unnamed *djinn*, and one particularly nasty *djenie*.

"I can't stand this thing one moment longer. You've got to get rid of it—right now!"

Sure enough, a grey-brown toad-like creature with three yellow eyes crouched at her feet. It's only human nature to start referring to a creature who accompanies you everywhere by name; people can't help themselves. And once a *djinn* has a name, they are forever attached to the person who names them. And once you've named it, it's nearly impossible to stop yourself from talking to them or giving them commands. Before you know it, they've become a permanent part of your life. Until death do you part.

I wanted to change out of my uniform. "Just give me a minute--."

"I've waited long enough! You have to help us." Others in the crowd echoed her frustration.

I held up my hands. "Okay, okay."

I'd been in exactly the same spot not so long ago,

and remembered how desperate I'd been to get rid of Blix. Demon masters are legally required to register with the government. They track the size of your demon annually, and any signs of growth indicate you've been using it for presumably nefarious purposes. Say good-bye to air travel, and probably your job, too. And unless your spouse files for divorce, child protective services usually moves to remove children from the homes of demon masters. In the eyes of the federal government, anyone who consorts or otherwise engages in naming, harboring, or summoning a *djemon* is guilty of terrorist activities. You can be arrested and imprisoned. And if they discover an unregistered demon of any size, you could be arrested and held without bail—or even executed.

Nobody wants that kind of trouble, which is why they go to the Hand of Fate.

And now, that's me. I am the last direct descendant of the goddess Morta, Queen of Death. Not exactly a super power, but having power over the non-living gives me the ability to banish pesky *djinn* and *djemons*.

I eased my way through the crowd to my front door. "I'll take care of each of you as soon I can."

There was a typed sheet of paper taped to my front door. An eviction notice. *Great*. The property had just been sold at auction, and I had to be out in 30 days. Not so surprising, really. My landlord had been jailed last month for having an unregistered demon, and no doubt needed to sell the property to pay for legal fees.

An old man peered over my shoulder. "I'll bet Mad Otto bought it. He's been buyin' ever'thing between Third and Bayshore. Gonna tear it down to make room for that blasted new Marina."

The old guy must've had chili with onions for lunch.

"Let's get on with it, girlie," chili breath grouched.

I crumpled up the notice and opened the door to my apartment. "The first two of you can come inside with me. The rest of you, please wait out here until it's your turn."

I climbed the stairs, accompanied by a pounding headache. After dropping my purse and helmet at the top of the stairs, I turned to face my first two clients. The first, a soccer mom, had a clear aura and deep maroon lifeline—sign of a normal human. On the other hand, chili-breath's lifeline was black. Curious, but not beyond my experience. It meant he was either not-human, or not-alive. Or maybe both.

My about-to-be new boyfriend, Rhys Warrick, didn't have a lifeline either. In his case, he was a *djenie*; a former *djemon* that had outlived his master. When his master died, Rhys was released from servitude and assumed a human form.

"Have either of you ever brought a *djinn* or *djemon* to Madame Coumlie to be banished before?"

They both shook their heads.

"Will it hurt?" Chili breath wore his long silver hair in a single thin braid that trailed down his back, past his waist.

"No," I bragged, "Doesn't bother me a bit. Piece of cake."

"I'll go get Mimsy," the soccer mom said, and she left before I could protest. *Great.*

Lying at his feet, the old man's *djemon* looked like a horned slug, and was about the size of a chocolate éclair.

"Come here little guy." When I reached out to it, it reverse halumphed away from me, out of reach. Golden eyes glared at me from atop dark eye stalks.

"Are you going to kill it?" The old man looked worried.

"No, no. It's not alive. It can't die. All I'm going to do is banish it." I took a deep breath, and shook out my sweaty hands. "Wait a second. What's its name?"

Chili breath reddened. "I swear I didn't name it on purpose. It—I started thinking of it as a Snot-wad, and before I knew it, that was 'er name."

Okaaay.

"Hear me and obey, Snot-wad. I am the Hand of Fate. I hereby banish you from all physical and metaphysical earthly planes, never to return." I clapped my hands.

Nothing happened.

"I command it." I clapped again. Again, nothing

happened.

"You have to hold his hand." Mimsy came into the room, accompanied by soccer mom.

"What?"

Mimsy grabbed my left hand and put it into the old man's bony right. "Now say it again. You don't need to clap."

"How would you know?" I felt like I'd just been scolded my one of my teachers, and it came out all huffy and pissy. I already felt like a stupid cow next to Mimsy, and having her tell me I was doing it wrong didn't help.

"Because that's the way Madame Coumlie did it for me the last two times."

She must have seen something in my face. "I'm just trying to help."

"Hey, you gonna fix this thing or not," the old man said. "I've gotta go to the can. I've been sittin' around waitin' for you all afternoon. I can't wait much longer."

"Sorry." I gripped his hand. "Okay then. Snot-wad, I banish you from all physical and metaphysical planes, never to return."

Immediately, an earth-shattering scream pierced the air. The windows rattled. We all put our hands over our ears, but Snot-wad's shrill wails and convulsions went on for several seconds before she finally blinked out. The old man snatched his hand away from me and grabbed at his chest. The echoes of the *djemon's* toe-curling squeals reverberated off the walls of my apartment for several long moments.

"Jaysus Mary of Morgantown. I thought you said it warn't goin' ta hurt. What in tarnation did you do? You some kinda sadist or somethin'?"

I stared openmouthed at the empty spot on the carpet where Snot-wad used to be. "I had no idea that would happen. They're not supposed to be able to feel anything."

"Feels like a piece been torn right outa me." The old man hunched over, his eyes watering.

Maybe he was having a heart attack. "Are you all right?" I reached for him, but he pushed me away.

"Don't know what yer tryin' to pull, here. Miz Coumlie never hurt anybody." He stumbled toward the stairs, muttering. "She never did no harm. Kept me comp'ny; me livin alone and all."

Soccer mom and Mimsy stared at me with wide-eyed apprehension.

"I didn't mean to hurt anybody," I protested.

"That never happened when Madame Coumlie banished my *djemons*."

"I don't think you're doing it right," said soccer mom. She had a death grip on her purse.

"Do you want to come back later?"

"I don't think that's a good idea." She pulled a scrap of newspaper out of the pocket of her jacket. "Have you seen this? It's from today's paper."

FBI Announces New Security Monitoring Measures for Selected US Cities

AP/UPI The Federal Bureau of Investigation announced that their Anti-Terrorism Task Force is beefing up homeland security efforts with specially-trained dogs to detect invisible threats such as demons, hexes, curses, and in some instances, compulsions. The dogs will be used at major transportation hubs such as airports, major rail stations, and subways to inspect travelers, pilots and engineers for psychic interference.

"We've known for years that dogs could be trained to detect drugs, explosives, and even diseases such as cancer. It wasn't a big stretch to train them to detect inhuman interference and demonic presence," stated an FBI insider on the anti-terrorism task force, who spoke on the condition of anonymity.

New York Senator Bob Wise (R) agreed. "The safety of the American public is of critical importance. These dogs can detect psychic and demonic interference at comparatively little cost to the taxpayer. The public is already used to seeing these dogs at airports, so it's not a big change. No one wants another incident like what happened in Europe two years ago. I for one, would feel much safer knowing that my pilot is not under the influence of some curse or demonic compulsion"

The first paranormal detection dog-handler teams were rolled out at the major international airports last year, but the FBI is also sending these specially-trained teams to selected cities where higher-than-normal incidents of supernatural activities have been reported. The FBI would not confirm or deny which cities have been targeted, but there are several small towns in Louisiana, Missouri, New Mexico, and upstate New York reporting recent spikes of supernatural activity.

I glanced to the top of the bookshelf, where my own two demons, Blix and Larry perched invisibly. They watched me with frightened expressions, their bulbous yellow eyes nearly popping out of their heads. So far, I'd managed to keep them hidden, but I wasn't so sure they'd be safe from a demon-sniffing dog. Maybe I should have banished them when I banished all the other *djinn*, but they'd saved my life, and I didn't *want* them to go.

"You think they're coming here?" I asked.

"My husband is a realtor. Two weeks ago he was

contacted by the FBI field office in Rochester. They're looking for short-term rentals that will allow dogs."

"Maybe it's for something else," I said. "Like search and rescue training or something."

"I'm not going to argue with you. I want this thing banished right now."

"Yes, but—."

"If the authorities find out, I could lose everything! I have children. I can't spend the rest of my life in hiding."

I could feel the heat of her fear radiating off her. Her eyes shone with anxiety. "Are you sure?"

She stiffened. "Whatever it takes. Just do it."

I looked at the lizard-thing crouched at her feet and swallowed hard. It had a single horn in the middle of its forehead. It was the first one I'd seen that really *looked* like a demon ought to. "What's the name?"

"No names," soccer mom said. "I don't want anyone to know who I am. And if you see me on the street, act like you don't know me. No one can know about this." She wrung her hands.

"No, I meant, what's your *djemon's* name?"

"Oh." She wouldn't look at it. "It's Barnaby. Can't we just get this over with?" Already Barnaby was looking a little uncertain. IIis big yellow eyes flittcd around the room, as if looking for a place to hide.

Poor guy. "Take my hand."

As soon as she touched my hand, Barnaby started

to squeal like a puppy. As I began to speak the words to banish him, the volume rose to an ear-splitting howl. A seizure gripped Barnaby, and a sour, scorched smell filled the air as he began to bite at himself, writhing in torment before he disappeared. It was an ugly, disturbing scene. Mimsy and soccer mom were both pale and trembling by the time the screams stopped. If there hadn't been a crowd outside, I would have run away right then.

Soccer mom snatched her hand back like she'd been burned.

"I'm so sorry," I gasped. I felt as if I'd just killed her pet. "Are you all right?"

She clasped her hands to her chest; tears streaming down her face. "It feels as if you ripped my heart out through my throat. It's like he was connected to me, somehow. Oh this is horrible!" She glared at me. "You murdered him, you evil witch!"

I tried to explain that Barnaby wasn't ever alive, but she only shook her head.

"I hope I never have to see you again." Her voice held the quaver of near-tears. She couldn't get away from me fast enough.

A moment later, the next client climbed the stairs and the traumatic scene was repeated. Each person as desperate as the last, each banishment an exercise in pain and anguish for both demon and master. And in the end, every one of them left furious with me.

I felt like a monster. I tried everything I could think of to avoid hurting the little guys, but nothing worked. Only two people showed up who had not yet named their *djinn*, and those were the only one which disappeared silently, like they were supposed to. Maybe the mere act of naming a *djinn* somehow hooked the creature into its new master. It was the only thing I could think of, because banishing the *djemon* seemed to cause too much agony for both of them. I wasn't sure if I could stand one more tortured scream.

If this was what being the Hand of Fate was all about, I wanted no part of it.

CHAPTER 3

FINALLY, IT WAS just Mimsy and me. Her *djemon* huddled miserably on my blue sofa beside her, as if seeking her protection. Blix and Larry peeked down at me from the top of the living room bookshelf, their eyes big as tangerines.

"We don't have to banish your guy," I suggested. The other *djemons* I'd banished appeared vaguely reptilian or like some sort of insect. Mimsy's looked like a wren-sized pterodactyl; with large frightened eyes and delicate little fingers. I didn't have the heart to hurt it.

Mimsy frowned and shook her head. "I don't have any choice. It's got to go. My brother's *djemon* ruined everything. If this one stays, it will destroy my whole family."

Or maybe there was really nothing different about Mimsy's demon. Maybe the difference was in me. I couldn't stand the thought of hurting anything so frail-looking.

"Look, they're easy to take care of, and they're so

smart. You don't have to feed them; they don't smell like the *djinn* do; they don't even poop. They're the perfect pet! I just tell mine to keep out of sight, and no one can see them but me. You could do that, too. I won't tell anyone."

"It's not that." Absently, her hands moved to encircle her demon protectively. The tiny creature seemed to relax into the warmth of her hands.

Somehow, I just had to convince her. "I originally planned to banish my *djemons* too, but they've really grown on me." Mimsy didn't have a lifeline. In Shore Haven, that meant she already knew how to keep secrets. It wasn't right. And from the way Mimsy was looking at me, I could tell she didn't really want to banish the poor sweet thing, either.

She shook her head. "No. This *djemon* affects the destiny of my entire family. Please don't make this any harder for me."

"What are you talking about? She's just one little *djemon*. Madame Coumlie had one, and no one ever knew."

"You don't understand. Look at this." She pulled up her shirt and pulled down the waist of her skirt to show me a large red birthmark.

"Yeah?"

"This is my family mark. It's the mark of the dragon."

I looked closer. It looked more like a snail to me, but what did I know? "If you say so."

"My family are children of the dragon." She straightened her clothes. "Our family legacy is entwined with dragons. My grandmother was a descendent of the vermillion lake dragons; she had the same dragon-shaped birthmark on her hip. My father, my older brother Joe, and I all have the same mark; the mark of Luhng, the red lake dragon. The blessing of the dragon bestows great good luck and benevolence to the families of their association. When I was little, Nana told me that when she came to Shore Haven, Luhng took one look at Lake Ontario, and was so pleased by what he saw; he decided to make it his new home. My family has been blessed by his presence ever since. Just as you have become the Hand of Fate, I am a Child of the Dragon. Like you, my life is predestined."

Yeah, right. You're cursed with luck. Boo hoo. *Try ruling the dead or banishing a few screaming demons and see how you like it.*

"If something happened to me, my entire family will be doomed. My father passed away two years ago, so my mother and Nana have taken over the business. I have two brothers. Joe is three years older than me, and by rights, he was the number one son. Just as my father carried the legacy of the dragon's luck and passed it from his mother to our family, Joe's destiny was to pass the luck of the dragon along to his children. It's the way it's always been for the children of the dragon. As long as we live under his roof, we all benefit."

Blix crawled down from his perch on top of the bookcase and settled into my lap. Blix's form is a baby sphinx. He isn't as skinny as he'd been when he first appeared. I tickled his hot little belly. He had new little nubs forming on his shoulders. Wings, I realized.

"Children of the dragon must be loyal to the dragon. But when Joe attracted a *djinn*, he kept Phantom secret from the family, knowing that we would disapprove. When Luhng found out, he began visiting all kinds of bad luck on Joe to warn him of the errors of his ways, but Joe didn't take the hint. The family business suffered. The restaurant had a fire. We were robbed. My father got the cancer. Joe said nothing.

"Finally, Luhng told Nana what was happening. She and my father made an appointment for Joe to have his demon banished by Madame Coumlie. Joe refused to go and ran away. Everyone was so angry. Two weeks later, we got the news that Joe had been killed in a car accident. A week after that, the cancer took my father's life. Luhng summoned Nana and told her that with Joe's death, the family legacy had passed to me and that if anyone ever again brought a demon into the family, we would forever be cursed by bad luck. So now, everything falls on me.

"Luhng's got my Ma consulting matchmakers in China. Can you believe it? A nine-thousand year-old dragon and my mother are going to pick out my future husband. I'm nothing more than a brood mare now.

My whole future is gone." She slumped miserably back into her seat. "You think I want to work at the House of Cards for the rest of my life? I've got a Masters Degree in finance! I could work anywhere! New York, Hong Kong..." Frown lines marred her beautiful complexion. "Joe was the one responsible for carrying on the family legacy, not me."

"Why does it have to be you?"

She looked at me as if I were an idiot. "I have the dragon birthright. I am number one son now. This is my destiny. I'm going to be stuck here in Shore Haven for the rest of my life, keeping the books in the back room and sending thugs out to collect the money owed to my family from welchers."

"No, I mean, what about your younger brother? Couldn't he take your place?"

"Kent doesn't carry the mark of the dragon. When Joe was number one son, I didn't care. I went to college. I made plans. But now, I must live close to the dragon. I can never leave." Her voice sounded bitter. She glanced down at her *djemon*. "I'm sorry, Annie. You have to go."

Annie.

I didn't know what to do. Not having had much of a family didn't mean I couldn't empathize. I didn't like Mimsy very much, but her story moved me. I couldn't bear the thought of banishing Annie, and I knew she didn't want to do it either. That put us on the same side. The words slipped out before I could stop myself.

"Maybe I could talk to the dragon."

Mimsy made a face. "Why would you even want to?""

Because I don't like being the bad guy. Because I can't stand the screaming. Because Annie hasn't done anything to deserve it. "Come on, at least let me try. I'm the Hand of Fate. Will one more day make that big of a difference?" *Because the thought of destroying that sweet little creature makes me feel like a monster.*

Almost as if she understood, Annie gave a mournful squeak.

Right then, I made a silent promise to do everything I could to keep from banishing Annie.

Mimsy sighed. "I can't think about this right now. I'm starving and could use a drink."

My stomach growled.

Warily, we eyed each other. "We could go together," I offered.

"Hurry up."

When I came out of the shower, she thrust a dark green sleeveless dress at me.

"I found this in the back of your closet. Don't you ever wear anything other than uniforms and sweatpants?"

I took the dress off the hanger and retreated into my bedroom to dress. "They're not sweat pants, they're play clothes," I hollered. I'd bought the dress on sale last year, thinking it would be perfect date dress, but no such event had showed up on my social calendar. Speaking of which, I hadn't heard from Rhys in two days. He'd told me not to make plans this weekend, but here it was Friday night.

I tried his cell phone, but he didn't answer, and his voice mail was full. I told myself he could be out of cell range or maybe he'd forgotten his phone, but all my excuses sounded lame to me. This was supposed to be our first weekend together. It was after nine o'clock already. Maybe he'd meant Saturday night.

I tried my brother again, but got no answer there either.

I shimmied into the short little green number and zipped it up.

"What's taking so long?"

Mimsy the dragon girl wasn't long on patience.

CHAPTER 4

WE CLUMPED DOWN the stairs of my apartment and out the door, then down the driveway and out onto the street toward a black Saab convertible with the top down. The night air sighed with a whisper against my skin; beneath me, the leather upholstery felt buttery soft.

"Where are we going?"

She started the engine, and the car purred powerfully as she pulled away from the curb. "You like Lapis?"

Never heard of it. "Where's that?"

She laughed. "You'll see."

I hoped it wasn't too far. The shower had refreshed me, and now all I could think of was food. I settled back into the seat, glad as anything to get the worst of this very long day behind me.

"Hey, we're going the wrong way," I told her.

Instead of turning right, toward Picston, Mimsy had turned left onto Bayshore, which skirted the lakefront and dead-ended at the breakwater, about two miles down. There was no business district out here; the street was lined with old summer estates and run-down mansions converted into condos and apartments.

"There's nothing out on the Strand."

Geographically speaking, the town of Shore Haven is shaped like dog's head with his mouth open. The tip of the dog's nose is the old amusement park, the tip of the lower jaw ends in a breakwater, which in the old days protected the town from wave action and high tides during winter storms. The inside of the dog's mouth is a manmade beach known locally as Horny Corners, where all the college kids hang out in the summer. Business men cruise by on their lunch hours, hoping to pick up a pretty girl, and there are always a few working girls on hand. When I was a kid, my mother was one of those women that walked the Strand. I didn't come out this way very often. No reason to.

I started to protest, but Mimsy cut me off.

"Wait for it."

The new marina plans call for tearing down every building on the lake side of Bayshore to make way for a private clubhouse, restaurants and boutique shopping. A lot of long-time residents of Shore Haven worry that the influx of new wealth will ruin the small-town atmosphere, but I'm looking forward to the day when the Strand and Horny Corners will be gone.

We were flying down Bayshore when the smell

of barbecue hit me. My mouth began to water. A new restaurant? I couldn't imagine where it could have been built; and I hadn't heard anything about it. We were almost at the turnaround at the end of Bayshore, when Mimsy made a quick right and drove us up the private driveway of one of the big estates. The aroma of barbecue hung thick as fog in the evening air.

This must be the place.

She turned right again and we were in a big parking area behind the main house. The huge residence loomed above us, silhouetted against the starlight. There must have been thirty cars in the lot, but I still didn't see any restaurant. Mimsy was grinning like a cat that swallowed a canary, as she sashayed past me toward the back of the old brownstone.

I hurried to follow her down the narrow path around the far side of the house. A high hedge grew over the walkway, blocking out the night sky. Strings of blue Christmas lights glowed in the dark foliage above us. In spite of the summer evening, I felt a momentary shiver of apprehension.

We reached a short flight of six steps that led down to a tiny landing. We faced an arched, narrow door, painted neon blue, set into the thick stone foundation. Mimsy knocked, and the door was opened by a large, fleshy bouncer with a shaved head and blue tears tattooed at the corner of each eye. A delicious aroma wafted out from behind his bulk to tantalize us. My stomach grumbled in appreciation.

"Welcome to Club Lapis, ladies. Nice to see you again, Miss Wu." He handed Mimsy a couple of tickets. "You and your guest are invited to accept these drink tickets, compliments of the house."

The basement opened into a lovely parlor, decorated in shades of beige and cream; a small bar to the left, a comfortable-looking seating area on the right. Thick Aubusson carpets, upholstered club chairs, potted palm trees, and floor-to-ceiling bookcases gave the room the look of an elegant library. Pinpoint overhead lighting lit the room from recessed alcoves, while the seating areas remained dim. It didn't look like any restaurant I'd ever seen. There was no one in the room.

"This way, Mattie." Mimsy motioned me toward a curtained archway, and when we slipped through, we were standing at the top of a stairway leading down into an open dining room.

I grinned. *It's a speakeasy.*

She led the way down the flight of stone stairs leading to the subbasement. On the jukebox, Muddy Waters wailed out an old tune from the 50's. The walls were of sandblasted brick and stone, with exposed fixtures and iron fittings. Black and ornately carved, the main bar ran almost the entire length of one brick wall, backed by a massive beveled glass mirror reaching almost to the ceiling, making the space look bigger. Fronting the kitchen, an open pit broiler dominated one end of the room; I could see several chefs and kitchen staff working at their stations. A row of smokers lined up next to a glass-walled distillery, full of copper equipment. Two dozen tables clustered in the center of the room; each festooned with white tablecloths and a small blue table lantern. Opposite the kitchen was a low stage and dance floor.

The whole thing fit together; it was tight and hip. I had the feeling we'd stepped back in time. The waiters wore long white aprons and bow ties. The cocktail waitresses stalked the room with voluptuous intent, brushing up against every patron they passed. The luscious smells of garlic and spices promised a memorable dining experience. The vibe was gritty, and a little bit naughty.

A fun place.

At the bottom of the stairs, the concierge greeted Mimsy like an old friend, and showed us to a table close to the stage. He seated us and motioned to a waitress to come over. "Lovely Dolores will be here in just a moment. Enjoy your evening, ladies."

Lovely Dolores herself arrived a moment later and proceeded to set down two empty glasses in front of us. Each glass was unusually-shaped, with a bit of a bulb in the bottom and a wide rim. She poured a clear bluish liquid from a glass decanter into each of our glasses, and then set the decanter on the table, along with a pitcher of ice water.

The anise smell hit me, and I was immediately

reminded of the smell of *djinn*. My empty stomach churned in disappointment as my appetite disappeared. Whatever it was, I didn't want any of it.

She laid a funny-looking slotted utensil across the top of each glass and rested a sugar cube on top of it. I glanced at Mimsy, but she looked as expectant as a kid getting served ice cream.

"What is it?"

"It is called La Bleu. It is our award-winning absinthe. We make it right here, the traditional way, using methods developed by the owner's family over two hundred years ago." Dolores slowly poured water from the pitcher over Mimsy's sugar cube and slotted-spoon arrangement. Mimsy held up her hand as the cloudy liquid in her glass reached the half-way point.

"That's perfect, thanks," she thanked the waitress.

I don't drink. Okay, maybe a beer at McGill's, but one is my limit, and I don't touch the hard stuff. My mother had been an alcoholic, and this stuff was strong enough to curl my nose hairs.

Mimsy removed the slotted spoon and took a large sip of the cloudy liquid. She smacked her lips. "You're going to love this, Mattie."

I held my hand over the glass. "No thanks. I'm not much of a drinker."

Mimsy handed Dolores our two drink tickets. "Oh come on. It's heavenly. You've got to try it."

Dolores smiled encouragingly. "Your friend is

right. The way we make it here, it's completely organic and natural. And the way we serve it, you can dilute it as much as you like." She poured the water slowly over the sugar cube until the glass was full. "Go ahead. Just a sip."

They were both staring at me, waiting for me. I didn't want to make a scene. If I was going to talk Mimsy into keeping Annie, I would need to keep on her good side. One tiny sip wouldn't kill me.

I took a tiny sip.

My entire body rebelled against it. My throat muscles spasmed shut; I couldn't swallow, even if I wanted to. I lifted my linen napkin to my lips and pretended to wipe them as I expelled the syrupy liquid into the cloth. "Mmm," was all I could say.

Satisfied, Dolores left us. I pushed the glass away from me, and watched as Mimsy took another drink.

"How can you drink that?" The smell of anise was all around us. "It's awful."

"I suppose it's an acquired taste. They say it's good for the blood."

Yeah, but who could get past the taste? My lips and mouth were numb, and Mimsy's eyes looked glassy already. It didn't take a fortune teller to see which way the evening was heading. I wasn't hungry anymore. If I started walking now, I could probably be home in twenty minutes.

"I should go." I started to get up, but Mimsy put

her hand on my arm.

"I thought you wanted to talk to Luhng."

"I do."

"What's your hurry? Relax. The music starts up in a few minutes."

"Um, I kind of had plans. I didn't think you were taking me to see Luhng *tonight*." I still hoped to hear from Rhys.

Something caught her attention behind me.

Coming down the stairs, was a tall, well-dressed black woman wearing a honey-blonde Tina Turner wig and a knock-em-dead figure. She was ginning like a cat that'd just finished the cream, strolling arm-in-arm with my almost-boyfriend, Professor Rhys Warrick.

My heart sank. It was *her*, it had to be.

Cavewoman Barbie. I'd never seen her before in my life, but her figure made her unforgettable. I should know, because Rhys had lent me a pair of women's custom coveralls from the back of his truck when we'd gone caving. On me, the top was embarrassingly big and the legs were about six inches too long; but they would've been a perfect fit for her. At the time, I'd been under the impression that Cavewoman Barbie was ancient history.

"Who is she?"

Mimsy squinted her eyes at them. "Doesn't matter," she mumbled. "Jus' the latest of a long list." She waggled her finger at me. "Rhys isn't who you think he is. Def-in-ite-ly not boyfrien' material." She finished the last of her drink and reached for mine.

I pulled it out of reach. "Come on, we're leaving."

"No. I wanna stay." The stubborn set of her mouth and her glassy eyes made me even more determined to get both of us out of there. She grabbed for my glass and took a long swallow, draining half the glass.

Rhys and the woman were standing at the bar with their backs to us. I put a twenty on the table and hoped it was enough. I pulled Mimsy's keys out of her purse. "Come on. I'll drive you home." I wanted to get out of there before he noticed us.

"All the women jus' looove Rhys." She managed to stand unassisted.

"You're not leaving, are you?" Dolores stepped out in front of us, standing much too close. "The show starts in a few minutes."

At that moment, Rhys and Cavewoman Barbie turned around and saw us. Rhys looked bleary-eyed and gave me no sign of recognition whatsoever. *Drunk*.

Heat rose in my cheeks. "Come on, we're leaving."

I put my arm around Mimsy's impossibly tiny waist and began making our way toward the stairs.

"You don't want to miss the show." Dolores gave me a big phony smile, but Mimsy had gone completely limp.

Time to go. I put my head down, got a good grip on Mimsy, and shoved our way past Dolores; but as soon as we reached the stairs, I felt a hand on my arm. It was cavewoman Barbie.

"I hope you're not thinking of leaving." She offered her hand out to me. "I'm the owner. I'd be delighted if you and your friend would join us at our table for the show."

The scent of rotting flesh and absinthe washed over me. There was something very wrong with her. Whatever she was, it wasn't human. I glanced at her hand. I did not want to touch her, or have anything more to do with this place. Or Rhys either, for that matter.

"Sorry, I think my friend is going to be sick. Maybe some other time." I grabbed the stair rail and dragged Mimsy upstairs and out the door with grim determination, fueled by an unreasonable need for escape.

By the time I poured the unconscious Mimsy into the passenger seat, I was shaking with fear, humiliation, and the sense of relief that we'd just barely escaped something terrible. Whatever I'd felt, or thought I'd felt for Rhys Warrick had dried up into a wad of revulsion. I started up the engine and we peeled out of the parking lot without a backwards glance.

CHAPTER 5

WHEN I WOKE up next morning, the couch was empty. Mimsy was gone. *Good.* Then I remembered my promise to help her. Hopefully, that wouldn't be too big a deal. That girl was nothing but trouble.

It was a little after noon on Monday when I stopped my scooter to write a ticket for an expired meter in front of the Paradise Garden Café. Mr. Yousef, who owns the place, has a very proprietary attitude about the parking meters in front of his restaurant. He doesn't appreciate people who park in front of his restaurant and then go across the street to get a coffee.

I had just tucked the ticket under the windshield of the late model red Audi when the car's owner came running across the street. He looked like a stock broker; expensive suit, Italian shoes, and red face. In the mid-day heat, sweat poured from his bald head.

"Don't! Don't! Please, I've got it right here," he panted, and leaned heavily against the car. His hand fumbled for change in his pocket, but he came up with nothing.

Mr. Yousef had come out of his restaurant, and was glowering at me from beneath his bushy eyebrows, as if to warn me against any sort of lenience, but it didn't matter. Once I write the ticket, I can't take it back.

When he realized he was too late, the guy in the suit seemed to sag. He sat down heavily on the pavement. His color wasn't good.

"Sir, are you alright?"

His face, so red only a moment ago, went deathly white and he keeled over onto his side. His lifeline was pinched tight in one spot and beginning to fade. I didn't know what was wrong with him, but I knew he was going to die without immediate attention.

I yanked my helmet off and shouted to Mr. Yousef to call 911; then knelt beside the man and felt for a pulse. His skin was clammy beneath my fingers; I couldn't feel a heartbeat. I loosened his tie, ripped open his shirt, then rolled him onto his back and checked his airway.

I'd taken my first CPR class in high school, and a refresher course offered by the Picston Police Department last year. But there's a world of difference between a rubber doll in a classroom situation, and a man lying on hot asphalt in the street. I started compressions. It seemed like forever before I heard the siren, and another eternity before the EMT touched my shoulder and relieved me.

I scrambled out of the way. The bitter coffee taste of him stayed with me. I hoped I hadn't made things worse.

The EMTs bagged him with oxygen and loaded him onto the gurney. I'd popped every one of the buttons from his fine shirt when I'd ripped it open. They tucked a blue blanket around him, which somehow made me feel better.

"Is he going to make it?"

The EMT shrugged noncommittally. "He's got a pulse. We're takin' him to St. Agrippa's. You can check on him there."

It was the best answer I was going to get right now. As the ambulance drove off, I made a silent wish that he'd be okay. With shaking hands, I brushed the dirt off my knees and thanked the Picston Police officer who retrieved my helmet and ticket pad.

Mr. Yousef shoved a white bag into my hands. "For you, Miss Mattie. My wife's special baklava. You saved that man's life. He could have died right in front of my restaurant!" His head bobbed. "Very bad luck."

I didn't know if I'd saved the man's life or accelerated his journey into the hereafter. I'd already killed one man by snapping his lifeline. At the time, it had been a choice between him and me, but the memory of that choice still haunted me. What if I accidentally snapped this guy's lifeline?

He still has a pulse, the EMT had said. I'd have to hold onto that thought until I finished my shift. The bus stopped less than two blocks from St. Agrippa's. I could check on his condition on my way home.

When I arrived at City Hall at the end of my shift, there was a WRPC television news truck parked out front and a crowd of people, a camera crew, and the mayor, Jim Brunson.

"Here she is," Mayor Brunson beckoned to me from the top of the stairs. "Our hero of the day."

Beside him, my boss, Mike, and the public information officer, Lacey Lippmann, stared at me with unhappy looks on their faces.

My heart leapt in my chest. "Is he okay?"

Brunson pulled me up to stand beside him, his arm around my shoulders. "Smile, Mattie," he whispered.

The newswoman pressed closer and the cameraman moved into position. "Just the Mayor and Mattie, please," She waved Mike and Lacy out of the shot. "It was a heart attack. The doctors say if you hadn't been there, Nick Durant would probably have died. He's going to be fine. How does that make you feel?"

Relief flooded through me. I grinned. "That's great! Glad to hear he's going to be okay." With Brunson's arm around me, I recounted what had happened, saying I hadn't known whether I'd actually helped him.

I don't remember what else I said. I rode the bus home in a happy fog. I'd actually saved somebody's life. I stopped in at St. Agrippa's on the way home, but they told me Nick Durant was still in ICU. His wife and son were there. She hugged me tight. I think we both cried a little. I'll never forget what she said to me.

"Bless you, officer Blackman. You're an angel."

Made me feel pretty damn good.

CHAPTER 6

WHEN I DID manage to fall asleep, screams of banished *djemons* haunted my dreams. I woke up with a start, but it was only a catbird mewling outside. I rolled out of bed, my eyes gritty, and my head pounding. I still hadn't heard from Lance, but when I got to work, Trusty Rusty was gone from the lot, and when I called the garage, Doc told me he was working on it.

Everyone at work had seen the interview on TV and when I walked into the break room at City Hall, I got a round of applause. Even Lacey Lippmann, the self-centered Public Information Officer asked me nice as pie if I'd give her an interview for the Mayor's monthly newsletter. I could tell it killed her to have to ask me, but I pretended not to notice.

Someone had pinned a picture of me and Mayor Brunson up on the bulletin board. The headline splashed across three columns:

Meter Maid Saves Syracuse Man
from Expiration

I'd never had my picture in the paper before, and it was a good picture; with me grinning like I'd just won the lottery. I'd taken my helmet off, and the camera captured my dark hair drifting out behind me in the breeze. I looked tan and athletic in my white uniform shirt.

I liked every bit of it. It felt great to be treated like a hero, and it had nothing to do with being the Hand of Fate and everything to do with being plain old Mattie Blackman. As I made my rounds that day, practically everyone I knew waved as I rode by.

Okay, yeah, without the ability to see Nick's lifeline, I might not have realized he was going to die, but that didn't matter. What mattered was the realization that I didn't have to live my life like my Madame Coumlie had. The whole Hand of Fate thing had been forced on her too, but in her day, women didn't have options. I could choose my own fate. Her legacy didn't need to define me.

I felt so good I stopped in at Dave's Killer Burgers for lunch and splurged on a bacon burger with extra pickles. Dave's is practically an institution in Shore Haven. In the fifties, it was a drive-through, but in the 70's they enclosed the place. Over the years, it's gone through several remodels, but never really strayed too far from the original maroon and turquoise tuck-and-roll décor. Their claim to fame is 100 different kinds of burgers on the menu and they serve breakfast twenty-four hours a day. The lunch crowd was already in full swing, but I managed to snag the last stool at the counter.

My landlady, Patty used to work here; at least until her ex-husband reported her to the FBI as a demon master. Now she was in federal prison awaiting trial, and I needed a new place to live.

While I waited for my food, I looked over the classifieds in the local paper someone had left behind. Mid-summer wasn't the best time to find a place, at least not in the Shore. Rents go sky-high, and all the cheap places get scarfed up by the end of May. Everything else was too expensive; even for a heroic meter maid. There were a few reasonably priced places over in Picston, but they were all in big apartment complexes, which didn't interest me. I needed a place with a private garage for my bike. And, come to think of it, Lance's too. He stored his racing motorcycles and some of this other stuff in the garage beneath my apartment.

Cindy brought my lunch and I dug in with gusto. Across the street, the sign for Mystic Properties caught my attention. That was Rhys's place. Officially he taught a few classes at the University of Rochester as a visiting professor, his specialty being ancient cultures. But in actuality, Rhys ran Mystic Properties as a sort of resource center for the paranormal community. He helped them find safe housing and forge identity papers to keep them safe from the feds. Maybe had cheap place for me too.

Or not. After seeing him with Cavewoman Barbie, I didn't know what to feel. Angry. Confused.

A lump formed in my throat as I stared at the CLOSED sign in the front window. I'd been so certain about him; I thought he'd felt the same way about me. I closed my eyes, remembering the feel of his hands on my bare skin.

Angry. Yeah, that was it.

"Excuse me, is this you?"

I jumped. A guy seated next to me at the counter. He was dressed in shorts and a tee-shirt, about my age, with blonde hair. He showed me the newspaper opened to the page with the picture of me standing next to the mayor.

I smiled. "Yep, that's me. Mattie Blackman." *This was so cool!*

"No, um. I mean, are you the one who banishes spirits? The one they call the Hand of Fate?"

I put my burger down and looked around to make sure no one was listening. Sitting on his shoulder, like a ghostly apparition, the guy's *djemon* gave me an unblinking yellow stare. I nodded, even as I groaned inwardly.

"I've got a little, uh, *problem* I need to get rid of."

I pushed my plate away. "I've got to warn you, it's not a very pleasant experience. Have you thought about keeping it?"

He frowned and shook his head. "No way. I can't

46

have this thing hanging over my head the rest of my life. Can you help me or not?"

He had dark circles under his eyes. Probably hadn't been sleeping well. Or eating either. Already, I could hear the future screams of his *djemon* echoing in my head.

I so didn't want this. I was going to *have* to find someone else to take over for the Hand of Fate. There had to be someone else who could banish demons. Surely there were other exterminators around. Maybe Henri would know who to talk to.

Henri Coumlie was no relation, but had inherited my great-grandmother's house. Although I was her heir, Madame Coumlie left her house and most of her money to Henri, and rightly so. For more than a century, he'd been her *djemon*; in the form of a sphinx named Oneiri. When she died, he became a *djenie* and assumed his immortal human form. Rhys was helping him to make the transition to living in society. I hoped Henri would remember how Madame Coumlie had banished her client's *djemons* and could tell me what I was doing wrong.

I gave the guy directions to Madame Coumlie's house and told him I'd meet him there after I got off work. When I went up to the cashier to pay for my lunch, I noticed two of Picston's finest, Bart Kitterman and Jason Jaekle, otherwise known as Heckle and Jeckle, sitting at their usual table near the door.

"Hey guys."

"Hey it's Mad Mattie."

Jason is the one with the mouth. His partner, Bart Kitterman, and I have known each other since kindergarten.

"Saw your picture in the paper," Bart said. The twinkle in his dark eyes just about made up for Jaekle's big mouth. "Way to go, hero."

"No shit, Mattie," Jaekle added. "You did good."

I thought he was kidding, but he wasn't. I was so surprised I didn't know what to say. I walked out of the restaurant grinning, more determined than ever to get my old life back. My old *friends* back.

CHAPTER 7

AFTER WORK, LANCE *still* wasn't answering his phone, so I took the bus home and banished a *djinn* and two *djemons* for the people who'd been waiting on my front porch for me. One of the women left crying. I didn't want to wait around for anyone else to show up, so I walked the three blocks over to Henri's house over on Empress.

A hundred years ago, Shore Haven had been built up around the Heavenly Shores Amusement Park, where Madame Coumlie had had been the headliner as a fortune teller. Most of the homes in town had been built around that time. The eclectic architecture in town included everything from huge stone lakeshore estates to Tudor brick to charming Victorian cottages. My great grandfather built the turquoise and lavender Queen Anne as a wedding gift for his new bride, and while it must have been lovely in its youth, it now stood out as a dowager painted lady, well past her prime.

But in spite of the peeling paint, weedy lawn and

the big hand-shaped fortune teller's sign out front, my feelings for the old place had recently softened. I stopped just outside the sagging picket fence and called up to a shirtless Henri perched atop a ladder, sanding the faded yellow trim around one of the upper windows.

"Whatcha doin?"

He turned and waved, then backed down the ladder to greet me.

"Hey, Mattie." He grabbed me in a hug tight enough to squeeze the breath out of me. "I think she's overdue for a fresh coat of paint, don't you?"

"What are you going to do about the sign?" For as long as anyone could member, the huge yellow sign had hung from the front porch:

DESTINY

BY APPOINTMENT ONLY

MADAME COUMLIE

He grinned. "Hey, the sign is the only thing that *doesn't* need painting."

It didn't seem right to keep that sign out front, but it wasn't my house, and I liked Henri too much to say anything that might hurt his feelings. "You got a minute?"

"Anything for you." He led me up to the deep front porch and lifted the lid on a Styrofoam cooler full of ice and bottled water. He offered me a bottle and I shook my head. He twisted off the top of the water bottle and drained half if it in a single long swallow. "What's the problem?"

I sighed. "There's a guy who needs to have his *djemon* banished. I told him I'd do it after I got off work, and told him to meet me here."

"No. I mean what's the problem between you and Rhys?"

"What? Why would you say that?"

"You've got a funny look on your face."

Not bad for a guy who had four legs and wings a couple weeks ago, but I didn't want talk about Rhys. "It's nothing. My car died and I need to find a new place to live."

"I can't help you with your car, but you're welcome to move in here with me." He waved his hand at the house. "It's too big for one person. There are five empty bedrooms upstairs. You can take your pick. People are used to coming here to see Madame anyway. It's perfect. She would have loved having you live here."

The absolute *last* place I would ever consider moving onto was the Hand of Fate's house. My goal was to *get away* from that life. "Um, I don't think so. I'll probably bunk with my brother for a while." I didn't exactly want to move in with Lance, but I didn't want to hurt Henri's feelings.

"But this place is perfect for you! I'll even repaint the sign." His eyes sparkled with enthusiasm. "You wouldn't have to pay rent. You could have the whole second floor to yourself, if you want. We could set it up any way you like."

Oh geeze. "Look, Henri, I already have a job. I appreciate the offer, but this whole demon-banishing bit is getting out of hand. It isn't what I thought it would be. I don't want to be Madame Coumlie's replacement. I have my own life to live. I don't want to be the Hand of Fate."

His face sagged. "You can't mean that."

Now that I'd said it out loud, I was more determined than ever. "Yes I do."

He took my hand. "You swore an oath to the goddess, Mattie. Her mark is on you." He turned my hand over and ran his fingers across my palm. Wherever his fingers touched mine, black runes rose to the surface of my skin, and then faded away. I shivered.

"Madame Coumlie felt the same way, sometimes. But when I touch your hand, there's a power there that surpasses anything Madame ever dreamed of. She was so impressed with you."

I pulled my hand back. "Don't say that. Besides, I totally suck at it. I can't even banish a *djemon* properly." I explained to him what happened.

"It's not that you're doing it wrong, it's that you're destroying the link between the *djemon* and their master. You have to be careful of the words you choose for the banishment."

"How am I supposed to know what to say?"

"If you lived here, I could teach you. And hey, you could teach me too! About being human, I mean."

"I thought Rhys was teaching you that stuff."

"He has been very busy lately."

"What kind of things you need to know?"

Henri's face lit up. "You could teach me to drive! And the Facebook. I need to know the Facebook. And chocolate chip cookies. I want to learn how to make chocolate chip cookies. Rhys does not know how to make them."

I laughed. "I could teach you those things without moving in."

"Madame also left most of her personal items to you. There are many boxes to go through. Perhaps you will feel differently about the Hand of Fate when you understand her legacy better. Many of the items are of great age and power. Things even Rhys hasn't seen."

"What kind of things?"

"Let me show you."

CHAPTER 8

HENRI LED ME through the house and down the stairs into the coolness of the basement. When he flipped the light switch, four bare yellow bulbs provided the only light. I gave a little yelp as shadows skittered across the linoleum into the darker alcoves on the edge of the light.

"What's that?" I'd seen similar creatures in the basement of St. Agrippa's hospital. Nasty things.

"Madame and Rhys have an arrangement. When the mortal master of a demon dies, often the *djenie* is too small to assume human form. Some of them are quite small and at risk of being preyed upon or eaten by local predators. The four small *djenie* living down here prefer the darkness. They will not bother us."

I looked around warily. "Lovely."

The basement was partially furnished. The walls had been painted pale yellow, but overhead, the 100-year-old ductwork, wiring, and pipes remained exposed. A couple of braided throw rugs decorated the floor, and to the left of the stairs, a maroon and black striped daybed squatted along one wall. To the right stood a washer, dryer, and stone sink set into a faux-marble gold and white Formica counter top. Opposite the laundry area, built-in cupboards covered the entire back wall; painted the same turquoise as the outside of the house. Piled in front of the cupboards, dozens of cardboard boxes had been stacked on top of each other.

Henri held his hands out to the boxes and cupboards. "This is all yours, Mattie. Madame wanted you to have it." He went to one of the cupboards and came back with something wrapped in a multicolored silk scarf.

He unwrapped the scarf and splayed a deck of small cards out in front of me. "These are carved of hippopotamus ivory. Very old. They do not look like modern Tarot cards, but they hold much power. They were her most prized possession."

The cards were nothing more than small rectangles of bone, each about twice the size of a domino, with primitive symbols carved into their surface. I shook my head. "I'm not a fortune teller, Henri. This kind of stuff means nothing to me. You keep them."

He rewrapped the cards and placed them back in the cupboard. "I cannot. You don't understand. This is your inheritance. She wanted you to have all of it." He pulled the lid off of one of the boxes and pulled out an orange and eggplant-colored tutu. "There are dozens of these; all one of kind. All made custom for Madame."

The tulle skirt was kind of cute, in a dry and dusty sort of way. This stuff would take me weeks to go through. "What am I supposed to do with all this?"

"Look at this." He opened another box and pulled out an oddly-shaped tool. It was about fifteen inches long, and appeared to be made with a single piece of scorched wrought iron; similar to a cross with a loop on one end and a hook on the opposite end.

"What's that?"

Heavy footsteps sounded on the stairs. It was Rhys. "Hey guys."

My body responded to the sight of him with an all too familiar tingle. I clenched my hands, determined to hold onto my anger. Mimsy's words haunted me. *All the women just looove Rhys.*

Rhys Warrick is the most unlikely-looking college professor I have ever seen. With a long black ponytail, Fu-Manchu mustache, black denim jeans and ass-kicker boots he's more biker dude than scholar, more mechanic than mage. Like Henri, Rhys is a *djenie.* Immortal; or close to it.

Definitely not boyfriend material.

Henri handed the implement to Rhys. "Madame believed it to be originally owned by Morta; the eldest of the three Fates."

Rhys ran his hands over the oddly-shaped cross. "Egyptian, I'd say. Legends say the Fates were Greek, but this predates Greece. I've never seen anything quite like it. Maybe an early *crux ansata*; sometimes called a handled cross; but this one predates Christianity."

Rhys turned it over in his hands, running his fingers over the inscription caved into the metal surface. "My best guess is an ankh. Symbol of life to the ancient Egyptians. Associated in symbolism as a gift from a deity, bestowed in the afterlife, which makes sense. But this hook looks more like the business end of an elephant goad. Interesting that the cross form is known as an *ankh*, the term used for the goad is *ankus* or ankusha. Call it a ceremonial ankh. Probably used in some sort of ritual."

Smile lines crinkled at the corners of his eyes. He held the ankh out to me. "Careful, that hook is sharp."

His bare lower arm was covered with bruises.

Hickeys.

Gross.

Henri grabbed his arm. "What happened to you?"

He grimaced and lifted up his shirt. Bruises covered his entire torso. The marks were more than love bites; the puncture marks of dozens of needle-like teeth perforated the skin around each bruise. "I woke up with them."

I couldn't stand it. "Don't play dumb, Rhys. I saw you last night, remember?"

"What?" Rhys gave me a blank stare. "Where?"

"At that jazz club at the end of Bayshore. Club Lapis."

"There are no clubs at the end of Bayshore."

"Yes there is. Mimsy and I both saw you there. *With a date*. Doesn't take a psychic to figure out where you got those bites." I shivered in the basement chill.

Henri and Rhys exchanged a look. "Mattie, I don't remember anything about last night."

"Yeah, right. She said you were her fiancée." It sounded like an accusation.

"This isn't the first time someone's reported those markings and couldn't remember how they got them. Are you saying you actually saw him?"

Rhys paled. "Mattie, tell me about the woman. What was her name?"

"I don't remember. She had an accent."

"What did she look like?"

"I know you know her. Six feet tall; built like a Barbie doll."

Rhys and Henri exchanged another look.

"Will one of you please tell me what's going on?"

Rhys took a deep breath. "Her name is Savanne Williams. She taught in the Geological Sciences department at the University of Rochester. She attended one of my guest lectures on indigenous cave art, and after the seminar, introduced herself to me, saying was an avid caver. She was married to an airline pilot who hated the idea of going underground, and since she wouldn't explore alone, she was looking for a partner to go caving with. I introduced her to a couple of people in the local cavers club, and she became a regular. Any time her husband was out of town, she'd join our treks. She kept her hobby a secret from her husband, so he wouldn't worry."

That explained why Rhys had her jumpsuit, but not the rest of it. I didn't know what to think.

"A few months ago, Savanne asked me to introduce her to Madame Coumlie. I set up an appointment but she never showed. The way she looks, people remember her. You're the first person to have seen her in months."

"Lucky me."

"Her husband reported her missing months ago. She is still listed as a missing person," Rhys said.

"Maybe it's not the same person," Henri said. "On the day of Savanne's appointment, someone left a card on Madame Coumlie's front door. Madame was deaf, and people often left notes on her door. The card was blank, except for the name, Savanne."

"There was something off-kilter about her," I admitted. "And the waitress too. All I wanted to do was get out of there." I shivered with the memory. "What's the last thing you remember?"

"I was on my way home to clean up for my date with you." Rhys said.

The heat in his eyes met mine and I blushed again. In spite of the ghastly marks on his body, I wanted to believe him. Wanted to have a private conversation. I wished Henri wasn't there. Instead, I forced myself to

look at the ugly bruises on his neck. *He's not human.
He's not for you.*

"I got a page from the building security company
about a possible break-in at Mystic Properties." He
paused, as if trying to recall the details. "I remember
driving over there, but I don't remember arriving."

My cell phone rang. It was Mimsy.

"Were you serious about talking to Luhng about
letting me keep Annie?"

Telephone manners didn't seem to be Mimsy's
strong suit. "Absolutely."

"I'll pick you up in ten minutes."

CHAPTER 9

I TOLD THE guys I had to go and raced back to my apartment. Blix was in his usual spot, curled up in an old knitted ski hat on top of the bookshelf, while Larry splashed and played in the kitchen sink. It surprised me how easily the three of us had adapted to each other.

Larry had the broad, ugly face of a Rottweiler married to the body of a stubby-tailed alligator. I didn't know what he was, but he sure loved the water. Since we were heading up to the lake, I decided to bring them both along. If Luhng saw how harmless they were, he might be inclined to let Mimsy keep Annie.

When Mimsy showed up, I realized I'd forgotten to ask Henri about how to properly banish djemons, but it didn't matter. I was done with the whole Hand of Fate thing, anyway. Annie would be my line in the sand. I started to ask Mimsy about the woman we'd seen at Club Lapis with Rhys, but she didn't want to talk about it.

As in *really* didn't want to talk.

By this time, I was more than a little ticked off by her attitude, but didn't want to push anything until I'd had a chance to save Annie, so we cruised up Third toward the old amusement park in silence.

Heavenly Shores Amusements had opened in 1906 and, for more than forty years, the park and its lakeshore access were a big draw for summer visitors from all over the northeast. The beaches were sandy and safe; protected by the breakwater we called The Strand, which was built up offshore and joined to the mainland.

In the 1950s, the New York State Thruway was constructed, and the Bayshore Drive off-ramp to the park was closed in favor of the Zoo Drive exit. Visitors to the park had to drive all the way around the Zoo to reach Bayshore Drive, which pretty much ruined the park business. Each year, the summer crowds thinned a little more, as there was nothing else to attract visitors.

It was a sad little place now; dying inevitably of neglect and decay. A tumble-down home to a few tattoo parlors, a dozen or so garishly-painted rides, and greasy food cart vendors. I hadn't been inside since junior high.

Mimsy parked in the near-empty visitor parking and I followed her past abandoned trailers and the pitiful midway. Overdressed, as usual, Mimsy wore a bright, skin-tight red wool suit, even in the high noon of a summer day. She had a wooden box under one arm, and strode purposefully down the cracked asphalt path toward the shoreline.

A security guard halted us as we passed through the nearly empty midway. I recognized him immediately as the former master of Snot Wad, the little slug-shaped demon I'd banished. He didn't look too happy to see me.

"Hold it right there, Missy. I want to talk to you."

Great. My first and most dissatisfied customer. He'd probably thought of a whole bunch of new stuff to tell me about how much I didn't know about being the Hand of Fate.

I glanced at his nametag. "Officer Crimmer. I'm with another client right now. Can this wait until we finish our business? It shouldn't take long." I gave him my most ingratiating smile, while Mimsy kept walking.

He frowned; his grey moustache quivered with what appeared to be agitation. Whatever he had to say to me, I knew I wasn't going to like it.

"All right. I'll be right here."

I ran to catch up with Mimsy, and caught her at the boardwalk, which ran along the lakeshore. In front of us, a cyclone fence loomed. It bordered the park, and ran out into the lake for a distance of thirty feet or more, most likely to discourage trespassers. She turned left and stopped at a secluded spot, screened from the rest of the park by manicured shrubs and a few large boulders, just short of the beach. On the other side of the fence, Bayshore Drive dead-ended, about a football field's length away.

Mimsy's agitation grew with every passing moment. She constantly tugged at her jacket and smoothed her skirt, picking at imagined bits of lint.

Across the way, something caught her attention on Bayshore Drive. I recognized the estate where we'd been earlier. The one that housed Club Lapis. She stared fixedly at the house, her jaw clenching rhythmically. I touched her shoulder. "Hey, are you all right?"

"I don't know what you're talking about." She slipped off her shoes and stepped off the boardwalk onto the spit of sand leading to the water.

I did the same. She stopped a few feet from the waterline, waiting, as the mosquitoes and sweat flies dive-bombed our hair. I looked around, but didn't see much of anything that looked the least bit dragonish. A bunch of empty cat food cans littered the boulders of the breakwater, where someone had set up a feral cat feeding station. It was peaceful here; the only noise was the small lapping of wavelets against the rocks.

"Where is he?"

She cupped her hands to her mouth. She let out a sound that was half-yowl, half-gargle. She paused, and did it again, then nodded. "He's coming."

Mimsy had told me that dragons were fierce negotiators. Any sign of fear or trepidation on my part would be interpreted as a sign of weakness. If I was going to have any credibility at all, I'd need to keep a cool head.

A stream of bubbles floated to the surface of the water from about thirty feet away and approached us. I glanced around for Blix and Larry, but they were busy sniffing empty cat food cans, invisible to everyone but me.

Luhng's head emerged first, a snarl of skin folds that reminded me of a little of a bulldog. Knots of convoluted flesh on the snout pulled his lips into a permanent grimace, exposing a mouth full of pointy teeth and tusks. Two dark, backwards-curving horns rose from each side of his forehead. His body, completely out of proportion to his massive head, was much smaller than I had expected; a snake-like body, followed by perhaps three feet of sinuous tail. He porpoised like an otter as he came to shore, all fluid grace until he touched the gravel. He was the deep color raspberry jam. Golden eyebrows perched above human eyes of pale green with a ring of gold around the pupil. His eyes looked just like Rhys'. In an instant, I realized that I knew what he was. Luhng was a *djenie* in animal form.

I am Djragon, a deep voice from inside my head corrected me. *I am eternal. I am god.* He slid ashore with surprising grace, and I took a step back as he emerged from the shallows on his two hind legs. The force of his energy hit me like a blow.

He stood about four feet high at the shoulder. Sitting up on his haunches, supported by his stretched out tail, seemed a perfectly natural act. He was both intimidating and comical. The deep red garnet scales on his back paled to sardine silver on his underbelly. A cushion of dense air surrounded him completely, like an invisible armor. I could not have stepped any closer to him if I'd tried.

"I greet you father, with affection and respect," Mimsy said, and bowed her head.

"Greetings child." The voice was as deep and resonant as the one I'd just heard in my head. "Did you bring my smoke?"

"I did, father." Mimsy opened the wooden box and lifted out a clay pipe with a long arching stem. She packed the bowl with aromatic tobacco, and held it out to him. Even with the long talons, his fingers were nimble as a monkey. He held the stem of the pipe to his ghastly mouth and puffed gently as she lit the tobacco for him. It was a ridiculous sight. I bit my lips to keep myself from gaping. He ignored me completely.

"Father, this is my friend Mattie--."

"Have I not provided you with all of the luxuries you could ever want?" He spoke gently, but the force of his personality was nearly overpowering. Mimsy dropped to her knees at his feet, unmindful of her beautiful suit. "Your family businesses are profitable. Your have benefitted from the finest education. Your health is unblemished. It is natural for my children to bear children. To strengthen our family and spread our prosperity far and wide."

Mimsy nodded; I could tell that this was a ritualized speech, one she'd heard a million times before.

"Your older brother has shamed the name of Luhng by taking a slave to serve him. The children of Luhng are not slaveholders. There is no need for mongering with such spawn of lesser godlets. You are the chosen one of my line now. Why are you not married yet?" Leung cocked his huge head at Mimsy as if he were considering the purchase of a new car. "You have a pleasant face. You are slim and lively as an eel. I would bless you and your mate with strong sons. Even a daughter, if you like. Why have you disobeyed me? Why are you reluctant to receive the bounty of prosperity that comes to all children of the *Djragon*? And more importantly, why have you insulted me by bringing the unclean spirit of a blasted *djemon* with you?"

Oops. I glanced toward the rocks where Blix and Larry were playing. Blix wasn't paying attention, but Larry had stopped everything and was staring at Luhng with the same intensity he normally gave me. I never should have brought them. I wanted to tell them to scram, but as I watched, Larry took a step closer to where we were standing. It was too late now; I could only hope that Luhng could not see them.

"It's not her fault," I protested. "Besides, *djemons* are neither good nor bad; they can do no harm without permission."

"Father," Mimsy reached out to stroke Luhng's,

er, hand. "The honor you seek to bless me with is more than I ever expected. It rightly belongs to my younger brother. I am a weak and spoiled woman, not worthy of your attentions. In Hong Kong, I have been offered a job--."

"What?" Luhng stood on his hind feet, and pointed at her with the pipe stem to emphasize his point. "Not this nonsense again. Is the water here not splendid? And the air. Is it not clean and fresh? And your father's garden. Is it not bountiful? Your family businesses prosperous? Why do you insist on returning to the Old World? The waters there are crowded and dirty. There is no reason for you to leave."

Mimsy bowed her head silently. Tears streamed down her cheeks. She trembled, curling up into herself. I couldn't believe this was the same haughty woman I knew.

"Why are you doing this to her? Can't you see she wants to live her own life? She has a right to make her own choices."

Luhng had a surprisingly expressive face. The look he gave me sucked the air right out of my lungs. "Silence. This is not your matter. I see the power you wield as the living manifestation of Death. The God you serve has a power that is greater than my own. But your words mean nothing," he sneered. "You are not of the *Djragon*. You know nothing of our ways. She must serve her destiny."

Movement behind Luhng caught my attention. To my horror, Larry seemed absolutely entranced by the sight of Luhng, and was waddling over to investigate.

"Listen, Luhng, this is America. Land of the free. Mimsy doesn't have to obey you, just because you want her to."

Mimsy waved her hands at me, trying to tell me to back off, but I was terrified that if I stopped talking, Luhng would notice Larry creeping up behind him. I had to keep the *djragon* focused on me. I was sweating now; I didn't know what Leung would do if he realized I had brought my *djemon*s with me, but I didn't think that I wanted to find out. I wracked my brain for something to say that would keep his attention on me. "Why won't you allow Kent to become head of the family?"

"Kent does not have the dragon mark. Miriam's mother and I have already selected a suitable mate for her. He will arrive soon—she could be with child by winter. Now banish her demon and be done with it."

At that moment Larry scampered up Luhng's leg and into his um, arms. As soon as Larry came in contact with the *djragon*, he materialized. Luhng's eyes widened in surprise. For a moment, he actually cuddled Larry like a puppy, before swinging him up for a better look.

Mimsy and I could do nothing but stand and stare at the *djragon* and the *djemon*. Larry was frantically trying to lick Leung's face, and for all his bluster, the angry *djragon* seemed charmed by Larry's efforts. I glimpsed a brief flash of delight on Luhng's face, before he settled Larry into the crook of his arm.

The red dragon pointed a taloned finger at me. "Look at what you have done," he demanded.

The weight of his presence and eyes forced me to my knees in spite of myself. I struggled to breathe. I had to think fast. I don't know why it hadn't occurred to me earlier--just as Blix was a baby sphinx. *Larry the Lizard was a baby djragon.*

Larry lounged happily on the dragon's arm; looking inordinately pleased with himself. I fought the instinct to send him and Blix back to my apartment. There had to be a way to use this to my advantage. When a *djemon* is released from servitude and becomes a *djenie*, if they are of a size, they choose a human form, like Rhys and Henri had done. Clearly, Luhng had chosen to retain his original form.

"I saved him," I gasped. "Rescued him from a fate worse than death. When I die, he will be free, just as you are."

"You have made him your slave."

His words were forceful, but all the heat had gone out of him. Larry's presence had him thinking differently about *djemons*, I could tell.

"I didn't do it on purpose, but yes. You're right. Until I die, he'll answer to me. But what is seventy or eighty years to an immortal? Even a hundred? It's nothing. If I banish him now, he'll drift forever in the nothingness between life and death. But if he remains with me, I'll spend the rest of my life being responsible for him; educating him, teaching him how to live and preparing him to survive as an immortal in a mortal world."

Luhng snorted. "What do you know of *djragons*?"

He set Larry down on the sand and the pressure which had kept me on my knees lifted. "Miriam holds the family legacy. She will bear many strong children. With each generation our destinies grow more prosperous and powerful. There has already been enough tragedy in this generation." He shook his massive head. "Joe's demon was an abomination. You must banish Miriam's foulness immediately."

I brushed the sand off my knees. "If I banish her *djemon*, it will tear a hole in her soul. Is that what you want?"

I looked around for her, but Mimsy was gone.

CHAPTER 10

EVEN HER SHOES were gone--and mine with them. Instinctively, I stared across at Club Lapis. I knew where she was heading, I should have taken her keys, but now it was too late. Something there had a hold on her that was more powerful than the dragon of prosperity.

Luhng roared his outrage. His tail thrashed angrily, churning up the sand. "You did this. You have interfered in my family." The pressure in the air around me began to build.

"No, wait! Let me talk to her."

The growl in his throat seemed to vibrate the earth beneath my feet.

"I know where she went; please, just give me a chance to talk to her," I pleaded. "Take Larry as my personal guarantee. I promise you I'll get rid of her *djemon* and bring her back. Just please; don't decide anything until I get back.

Luhng didn't say anything, but the growling stopped.

"Larry, I command you to stay with Luhng. Do everything he says, until I tell you specifically not to." Larry didn't make a sound, but he blinked at me with what I could only hope was acceptance. He slithered over to Luhng without hesitation.

"Good boy." Too late now to change my mind. "He likes having his belly rubbed."

Without a word, Luhng turned toward the lake. He reached the water in a few ungainly steps, and then leapt forward, diving onto the water. Larry, who was much more agile, raced forward, and swam strongly beside him, using his tail to propel himself through the water. I watched them until they disappeared from sight. Larry never looked back, not even once.

I sighed. Better get this over with. I knew exactly where Mimsy was headed, but it was a good twenty minute run to reach the house that was less than two hundred yards away. I'd left my cell phone in her car.

The park's perimeter fence was topped with barbed wire, but the fence ended about fifty feet into the lake; less than half a lap in the Olympic-sized pool at the Y where I swam five days a week. I raced to the water and jumped in.

CHAPTER 11

I DON'T THINK it took me more than five or six minutes to swim around the fence and reach the big stone estate that housed Club Lapis; but when I got to the parking lot in the back, Mimsy's Saab was already there. She'd locked my shoes and cell phone inside. I cursed and ran around the side of the house to the basement entrance of Lapis.

I pounded on the door several times, but no one answered. Maybe it was too early for them to be open. The neon sign and twinkle lights weren't on, but I could feel the throbbing of drums vibrating through the thick door. There were no ground-level windows. She *had* to be in there.

Soaking wet, I ran around to the front door of the house and rang the buzzer. I pounded. I shouted. Still no answer.

There were four other cars in the back parking lot, but they were all locked, too. Something bad was about to happen to her; I just knew it. She hadn't been acting normal. I had to get to a phone.

In desperation, I pulled off my still-wet tee-shirt, wrapped it around my elbow, and tried to smash the window of the Saab. I must have tried half a dozen times, but that safety glass was tough; I couldn't break it. I looked around for a big rock. I finally managed to wrest a loose brick from a crumbling retaining wall. It took me two tries, but I finally managed to smash the passenger's side window.

The safety glass exploded and the car alarm went off. I winced at the noise, but at this point, there was no turning back.

I reached in through the window and scooped my sandals off the front seat. No sooner had I slipped them on and dialed 9-1-1, than a Picston black and white pulled into the parking lot with lights flashing. Thank goodness.

I shouted and ran toward the car. "Over here!"

The car slid to an abrupt stop and two officers stepped out of the vehicle. They raised their weapons. "Halt!"

I recognized them immediately. It was Lou Scali and his rookie partner, Wes Zigo. "Lou! What a relief. Thank god you're here. Call for backup. A woman's been kidnapped. She's being held inside this house!"

"Mattie?" Lou holstered his weapon and motioned to Zigo to do the same. Both of them shook their heads at me, grinning ear to ear. "Where's the party, girl?"

I suddenly realized why they were staring. I was wearing only a pair of soaking wet shorts and a bra.

"Oh crap. Just a minute." I ran back to Mimsy's Saab and picked up my shirt, but it was covered with shards of broken glass. Lou and Zigo were right behind me. I held the glass-filled wet tee-shirt of me, while at the same time tried not to let it touch my skin.

"What's going on here? We got a report of someone breaking onto cars over here. Looks like you're it."

I groaned inwardly. "This is not what it looks like. My friend and I were over at uh, the amusement park, and um, she left without me. I followed her over here, but they won't let me in." Both men were giving me serious cop face. "She's in trouble, Lou. She's not herself. We need to get her out of there. I don't know how many of them are in there." I looked around the lot. "At least three or four; call for back up."

"Did you do this?" Lou nodded at the broken window.

Oh jeeze. Whatever I said, I was not going to like the outcome of this little conversation. Don't get me wrong, I love and respect cops. I grew up wanting to be a police officer, more than anything else on earth. Some of my best friends are cops.

"Earth to Mattic. Come in."

I took a deep breath and struggled to keep the rising hysteria out of my voice. "It was an emergency. My phone was locked in her car. I was trying to call you guys." I looked at Scali, but his eyes were on something behind me. I turned, and was surprised to see the woman I'd seen with Rhys the previous night, and the bald bouncer approaching. In a low voice, I said "That woman is the one who is holding my friend. You've got to help me get her out of there. They're keeping her against her will."

I had to admit, things were not looking good. She was dressed to the nines in white linen slacks and four-inch heels. She was wearing a different wig than I'd seen her in before: this one was a mass of black curls. She had on a wispy voile top that showed off plenty of cleavage, and dark sunglasses. Next to her, baldy the bouncer was wearing an obviously expensive suit, and several gold chains. Together, they looked hip and trendy. Lou told Zigo to stay with me, and he went over to talk to them.

I didn't hear what was said, but there was quite a bit of the three of them looking at me and talking.

"You the one they call Mad Mattie?" Zigo asked.

I ignored him. Zigo had been on the job less than two months.

"Don't be thinking you're getting out of this just because my partner knows you. You're in a boatload of trouble, lady."

"You don't know what you're talking about."

"Looks to me, like we've got you on attempted grand theft, B and E, vandalism, and trespassing, for starters." He leered at me, trying to get a better look at my wet bra, which to my horror was practically transparent. "Who knows, maybe even a morals charge for public indecency."

Lou motioned to his partner to put me in the back of the car, and followed the woman and Baldy back toward the house.

Zigo tried to get me to sit in the back, but I refused. "I'm not going anywhere, and I haven't been charged. I'll sit in the front, but you can't lock me in the back seat. Go on; back up your partner. Those people have got my friend. I'll wait right here"

He started to argue, but clearly didn't know what to do. "Don't touch anything."

Rookies. Ten minutes later, Scali and Zigo returned. "You need anything else from that car, Mattie?" Scali handed me my cell phone and nodded toward the Saab.

I shook my head. "Where's Mimsy?"

Scali started the engine, and Zigo slid wordlessly into the back seat. "Your friend Miss Wu told me she did not want to press charges against you for the damage to her car." Scali turned in his seat to look at me directly. "She also told me that you are not friends. The Sinaloas have declined to press charges, and have asked me to escort you off the premises. Both Miss Wu and the Sinaloas claim you have been stalking them. I advised them that if this was a problem, they can get a restraining order issued against you."

Stunned, I could only stammer. "But--."

Lou put the car in gear. "I'll take you home."

I grabbed his arm. "Wait. Lou, you've got to believe me, there's something going on in that house." I caught a smirk on Zigo's face in the back seat. "Aren't you even going to investigate?"

"Look at you Mattie; you're a mess. Be glad I don't take you in, because believe me, the next time I will. There is nothing I can do. This is private property."

"What about the club? They're selling liquor without a license."

"What club? Have you purchased any alcohol here?"

This was going nowhere. "No. They gave us free drinks," I mumbled.

"That's not illegal," Zigo piped up from the back.

How could everything have gone so wrong? I slumped in my seat, shivering in the air conditioning.

"For what it's worth, Mattie. I don't believe a damn thing I heard from any of them. Something is not right with those people, but without probable cause, there is nothing I can do."

"I understand."

"I hear you're old lady Coumlie's heir. I saw you at the funeral." Scali's eyes met mine. He didn't have a lifeline, I realized. The ability to see people's lifelines and auras was still new to me. I'd been spending so much time around Rhys and Mimsy and Henri, I'd stopped noticing when people didn't have them. But Lou Scali was a cop; and apparently not an entirely human one, at that. *Interesting*. All the more so because not one of my friends in the department had come to my great-grandmother's funeral. For Scali to say he'd been to the funeral meant something.

Lou Scali had something to tell me.

"That's right." I held his gaze. We understood each other.

"Maybe there is more going on there than meets the eye. All I know is that right now, it's not cop business. *We can't help you.* Understand?"

I nodded. "Yeah." I licked my lips. "Yeah, I do."

He pulled out of the parking lot and headed over to my apartment.

We heard the sirens from three blocks away, and as Lou turned the patrol car onto my street, the smoke billowed out to greet us.

I opened the door and raced up the sidewalk, through the crowd and past the barricades, but there was no mistake.

The fire trucks were parked in front of my place.

CHAPTER 12

THREE HOURS LATER, my landlord Patty's house had been reduced to charred black ruins. Fortunately, the carriage house in back of the lot was built of stone. The only damage was to the roof, where a stray spark had landed. As his men rolled up the hoses, the fire chief, Bud Eckersly, told me I wouldn't be allowed onto the property until after the arson inspection.

I argued. I begged. But Eckersly wouldn't let me back into my apartment. He loaned me an old t-shirt with the words, "FIREMEN DO IT WITH BIGGER HOSES" emblazoned across the front. Then he handed me a card with a number for the Red Cross and told me to get back behind the barricades.

My eyes and throat burned from all the smoke. I shoved my card into the pocket of my shorts. *Great*. No house, no car. Nothing but the clothes I was wearing on my back and my cell phone. I called Lance, but he still wasn't answering, and his voice mailbox was full. *Double great*. Lucky for me he lived only a few blocks away.

I started walking. Lance lives in a tiny two-bedroom brown bungalow on St. Clement, bordered by the alley that runs along the business district along Third Street. It's a rental, and Lance isn't much of a gardener, so the postage-stamp-sized front yard isn't as well-tended as the other houses on the block. The sun was dipping down toward the horizon as I walked up the three steps to the front porch.

The pile of newspapers in front of his door told me how long he'd been gone. More than a week.

I used the spare key hidden behind a bit of trim around the front window to let myself in.

The place was empty.

Not just empty of Lance, but stripped of every stick of furniture, every tattered rug, and every shred of paper. The bare floors echoed hollowly as I went from room to room, checking the closets, cupboards, and even the refrigerator. He was gone.

Numb, I slid down the wall to the floor. I couldn't believe Lance would have packed up and left town without telling me. I struggled to remember our last conversation, at Madame Coumlie's funeral. He seemed okay. He'd just been let out of jail, and had come to pay his respects. They'd been friends; he hadn't known she was our great-grandmother. I hadn't known he'd had a *djemon*. He'd hidden it from me, just as I'd hidden Blix and Larry. We'd been keeping secrets from each other. He'd started gambling again, and I'd told him he had to go back to rehab.

His parting words to me rang in my head. *See you around, brat.*

Maybe that's what he'd done. I don't know how long I sat there and argued with myself. By the time I was all cried out, I'd pretty much convinced myself that he'd put his stuff in storage and checked himself into a residential rehab. But as hard as I tried, I couldn't quite make it work. He would have told me. Or his partner, Doc. Or his ex-wife, Violet.

I needed to talk to them.

CHAPTER 13

THE SKY WAS pink and orange with the vibrant colors of sunset by the time I got back to Henri's, where a half-dozen impatient clients waited for me in the front parlor. Oh geeze. I'd completely forgotten about them. Barefoot and still dressed in that ridiculous tee-shirt, I'm sure my appearance didn't inspire much confidence.

I told them I'd be right back and dragged Henri into the kitchen. "Tell me how to banish their *djemons*."

"You think banishing a *djemon* is the same thing as banishing an unnamed *djinn*. An unnamed djinn has no master, so banishing it is easily done. Once accepted by his master, a djemon's spirit becomes deeply rooted within his master's soul. It's like a fish hook. You are much more powerful than Madame was. When you banish a named *djemon* in the same manner as you banish a *djinn*, you brutally rip the djemon's spirit from its master's soul. This destroys the *djemon*, but it also leaves a gaping hole in the soul."

I cringed, thinking of the damage I'd done.

"Madame Coumlie was only capable of banishing demons from the physical plane. By doing that, they are still joined with their master, but can never materialize in the present. Since they are no longer capable of obeying their master's corporeal requests, they never grow. Thus, when its master dies, the *djemon* perishes as well."

"Got it." I kissed his cheek. "Thank you, Henri. You're a life saver."

This time, there were no screams; only the effusive thanks of grateful clients. Henri congratulated me, saying Madame Coumlie couldn't have done a better job. Just after the last client left, Rhys arrived.

The poisoned bites he had received earlier had nearly faded, leaving only the faint outline of pincushion teeth marks where they'd punctured the skin. I tried not to stare; the sight of them sickened me. I still wasn't certain whether I believed him or not.

I told them about Mimsy running away to the Club Lapis estate, the police, and Mimsy's refusal to come out of the house. Then I told them about the fire and finding Lance's house empty.

"Can I stay here for a few days Henri? Just until they let me back into my apartment?"

"This place will always be your home too, Mattie," Henri said. "As far as I'm concerned, we're family."

I kissed him on the cheek. "Thanks, Henri. But I'm not a very good sister. I've already driven Lance away. He didn't even leave a note."

Rhys made a face. "That doesn't sound right. Lance adores you, Mattie. Come to think of it, Savanne didn't leave a note either. Her husband came home from a trip and she was gone. A week later, he got a postcard from her, telling him she wasn't coming back. The police thought it was just a family thing, but I'm not so sure. Have you gotten a postcard from him?"

I shrugged. "I haven't checked the mail in a couple days, but--."

"Mattie, listen to me. This is important. Before Savanne disappeared, she had an appointment with Madame Coumlie. I think she had a *djemon*. I know you can see *djemons* that aren't on the physical plane. When you saw that woman last night, did she have a *djemon*?"

I thought for a minute. "No, now that you mention it. I did see a couple of *djinn* that night, but they were in the company of other customers. Other than Mimsy and myself, I didn't see anyone that worked at the club with a *djemon*." I tried to remember what else I'd seen that night. "Although, come to think of it, I don't think anyone we saw had life lines." A feeling of unease welled up in me.

"Is anyone else missing? Maybe there's a pattern." I hoped so, if for no other than selfish reasons. I didn't want to think that I'd driven Lance away, but the alternative wasn't much better. He might have started gambling again, but what if something had really happened to him?

We made a list. In addition to Mimsy and Savanne, Henri and Rhys came up with ten more names. Eleven, if we counted Lance, but I wasn't sure they were right about Lance.

"That's a lot of people," I said. "How can so many people disappear and not be noticed?"

"It's not that they haven't been noticed. But only half the people on this list are human. Lance didn't have an appointment with Madame Coumlie because he planned to keep Jinxsey. But he's the only human who hasn't been reported missing yet."

Jinxsey. That was a name I hadn't heard in a long time. The black stray cat we had when we were kids.

"The others are anomalous individuals like Mimsy. We try to keep a low profile, so if one of us goes missing, you can be sure that no one is going to report it."

"So how many on this list are *djenies*?"

We went through the list. None of the anomalous individuals who had disappeared were *djenies*. As far as we could tell, all the missing had made arrangements to have their *djemons* banished by Madame Coumlie, but she died prior to their appointments. The only exception was Lance.

"Sounds to me like someone is targeting demon masters."

Henri looked scared. "Do you think they're coming after *djenies* too?"

Rhys shook his head. "I wish I knew. None of this

makes sense."

"Maybe they decided to go somewhere else to have their demons banished," I offered. "I mean, that's what I did. Or tried to do. Maybe they found a place that could banish their demon sooner."

Rhys shook his head. "Every exterminator in town brought their client's demons to Madame Coumlie. She's the only one who could actually banish them from the physical plane."

A knock sounded at the door. A moment later, Henri returned with the security officer from the amusement park, still in uniform. "Charlie Crimmer wants to talk to you, Mattie."

The one whose *djemon*, Snot-wad, I'd banished earlier. The one I'd stood up.

I jumped up, blushing. "Oh gee, I completely forgot--."

He made an abrupt, slashing movement with his hand. "You did somethin' to me. I don't know what, but I can't do my job no more. Without my job, I'm nothin'." He patted his chest and spread his arms wide in a dramatic gesture. "I always thought the Madame would be the one to send me on, but I was wrong. Since you're the new Queen of Death, you might as well do it now."

Like the Hand of Fate wasn't bad enough. Crimmer's black lifeline glowed darkly. I wondered, not for the first time, why. I had no idea what he was talking about. "Tell me what's wrong."

"I can't do my job." He patted his chest again. "How can I provide a safe passage for souls when my own isn't whole anymore?"

Baffled, I looked to Rhys and Henri. "Do you know what he's talking about?"

"Charlie guides the souls of the dead through the portal from the physical plane to the astral plane." Rhys explained. "Shore Haven is located on top of a gateway between the realms."

"Madame Coumlie hand-picked me for the job. Now she's gone and everything's gone to shit." Crimmer glared at me with unveiled disgust.

"How does it work?"

"Well I don't hold their hand, if that's what you mean. I maintain the portal. You know, keep it clear, and make sure none of the ones already crossed over can come back. The souls flow through as long as I'm there to keep it safe. But that's what I'm tryin' to tell ya, I can't do it anymore. You tore something outta me. It's sucking at the souls of the departed; they're scared to come by me now. They ain't flowing proper. And the ones that do get past, ain't staying over there. I can't do it no more. Ya gotta get somebody else."

I turned to Rhys. "Can you--?"

"Nope. And neither can Henri. Neither of us are human. We don't have souls. Charlie is a spirit guide; descended from the shamans of the original indigenous tribes of the area."

As I looked beneath Charlie's wrinkled uniform, the proud heritage of his ancestors became more obvious. Prominent cheekbones, a broad, flattened nose, and strong jaw gave him a pleasant, if stubborn-looking appearance. His eyes were so dark as to be almost black, but held an inner gleam of wisdom. I'd made a snap judgment about him based on his age, his lack of laundry skills, and what he'd had for lunch.

I'd been making a lot of mistakes lately.

"I'm sorry, Mr. Crimmer. I don't know what to do." I appealed to Rhys. "I have to fix this. Isn't there some way to heal a torn soul?"

"I don't know. The soul is a delicate instrument. Charlie's soul is trying to mend itself by grabbing onto the souls of the recent dead. It explains why the souls seeking passage to the next plane are wary of him. He cannot be allowed to remain at his post." He nodded to Charlie. "Sorry man. I don't have the answers, either. I'm going to have to research this."

Thankfully, Rhys's area of expertise is shamanism. He came to Shore Haven from Scotland to study the indigenous peoples in the area; specifically, the local Seneqouis legends. If anyone could find a way to undo the damage I'd done to Charlie's soul, it would be Rhys.

"We cannot leave the portal unguarded." Henri said.

"Aye. That's what I've been sayin'."

"Um, where is it, exactly," I asked. "And who's watching it now?"

"It's beneath the Funhouse," Charlie answered. "We got regular hours, but I closed it up today, on account of what happened, and came looking for you. When I saw the barricades around your apartment, I didn't know where else to go."

"So what's the problem?"

"When I shut down the portal, the souls don't know where else to go. I'm sayin' we got a bunch of lost souls wandering 'round Shore Haven."

CHAPTER 14

I DREAMED OF our old cat Jinxey. A scrawny black-and-orange tortoiseshell that showed up on our front porch one day and stuck around for six months until she got hit by a car. I was still in braids; second grade, I think. I ran back home to tell Lance, who gathered up what was left of her in a garbage bag. We lived in an apartment, so Lance dug a hole beneath an azalea bush in Doc's parent's back yard. Lance cried even more than I did when we buried her. For weeks afterward, we kept thinking we heard her crying at night. Such a loud meow for such a little cat...

I woke up in a strange bed. Morning sun streamed through the voile curtains; filtered through the leaves of a large ginkgo tree outside the window. It took me a minute to realize where I was.

The Green Room, as Henri called it. Directly above Madame Coumlie's reading room, the windows on the curved walls of this turret-shaped bedroom overlooked Empress Street. Henri told me this had been my grandmother Oleana's room, when she was a child, but that had been long ago. Oleana had run away from home as a teenager, and the room was rarely used. The décor was simple vintage; a mirrored oak armoire, a couple of small bedside tables, and an overstuffed wing chair upholstered in a pink flowered fabric. And the bed; a sturdy iron affair wrought with doves and roses and painted white. Definitely a girlie bed. I snuggled deeper beneath the quilted coverlet.

Charlie Crimmer stayed until after midnight. He agreed to keep the portal shut down for a few more days until Rhys could find a way to heal his soul or we could find someone to take his place for a while. Rhys had left to check the university archives and to do a little research on soul mending.

I was going to need something other than that fireman's tee-shirt to wear. I figured I'd sneak back to my place and pick up some stuff, but as I headed downstairs, someone was ringing the front door buzzer.

"Is Madame Coumlie in?" A well-dressed, older woman, probably in her fifties stood on the front porch.

"I'm sorry. She recently passed away."

"Oh dear. I'm sorry for your loss." The woman smoothed her salt-and-pepper hair. "Perhaps there is some else you could recommend? I've been coming to Madame for more than twenty years. Finding a psychic with real ability is so difficult these days. Perhaps someone else *in the community*?"

It hit me then. This woman probably wasn't the only person who had long-standing appointments with Madame Coumlie. Surely there was some kind of appointment book. I needed to notify them; give them someone else to go to.

I took her name and phone number, and told her I couldn't make any promises, but that I would try to find someone else. Of course Madame Coumlie did more than just banish *djemons*. She told fortunes too. And who knew what else. With that big-assed sign out front, people would keep coming to the house looking for her; looking for help. I needed to get organized. We needed some kind of referral service. We also needed to take down that sign.

I don't have time for this. I needed to find a new place to live. Staying here was out of the question. The longer I stayed, the more people would expect me to be the Hand of Fate. And that was so not going to happen.

Ten minutes later, the doorbell buzzed again. This time, it was a street kid, by the looks of him. No life line. He'd hitchhiked from Buffalo looking to buy citizenship documentation. That was Rhys' area of expertise. And illegal. But at the same time, the kid had a desperate look about him that haunted me. Looked barely fourteen, but no way to tell; he could have been centuries old. I told him about Mystic Properties, and said that if he couldn't get hold of Rhys, to come back the next day.

By the time Henri got back from the hardware

store, four more people had showed up; only two of which needed their *djinn* banished.

"Henri, this has to stop. We need to contact her clients and let them know she's no longer available. And we need to take down that sign."

Henri took me into the kitchen and showed me the list of a dozen phone messages from people looking to make appointments with the new Hand of Fate. "You are the Hand of Fate now, Mattie. These messages are for you. You have to help them."

"Hey, I'm no fortune teller. I've already got a job, get it? And where's her client list? We need to call these people and notify them that their appointments have been cancelled. And I guess we ought to find another fortune teller to send them to. Wasn't Rhys planning to take over for her anyway? Why can't he take care of all this?"

Henri led me back into the parlor. In spite of the high ceilings and large window, the circular room retained its cave-like, mystical character. Purple and orange flocked wallpaper covered the walls; runes, stars, and mystical symbols encircled the doorways and windows; the walls were covered with sepia-toned photographs and bits of ephemera from her life. This room, more than any in the house felt most powerfully of her presence.

He showed me her computer. "I have not yet learned how to use it," he admitted. "She was deaf, so most of her clients contacted her through email. I am certain there are many more messages here.

Just being in the room reminded me so much of her, and what I didn't want to become. I powered up the PC, but could not access any of her files without a password, which Henri did not know.

"If Rhys was originally planning to take over for her, wouldn't he have a copy?"

Henri nodded. "I believe you may be right. Rhys keeps a mailing list for the anomalous community; it is likely that Madame gave him her contact list for her human clients as well."

"Agreed. So we'll talk to Rhys when he gets back. Is there someone in the community who she might have recommended?"

"I know you don't believe it, but I would encourage you to explore your new powers, Mattie. You are more powerful than Madame ever was. No doubt you can serve her clients as well as she did."

My great-grandmother's reading table and chairs were situated right in front of the big picture window. For as long as anyone could remember, Madame Coumlie had sat in that window, telling fortunes. Her clients were screened from view by the voile curtains, but my great grandmother wasn't shy about letting the people know when she was working. I shuddered and vowed to start interviewing the local fortune tellers as soon as possible.

"No way. I've already got a job."

CHAPTER 15

I TRIED CALLING Mimsy, but there was still no answer. I called Lance too, with no better results. Maybe Rhys and Henri were right. Maybe Lance's disappearance was connected with the others. I shook my head. *He's gone into rehab, that's all.* In a few weeks he'll be back. *If only I could be sure.*

I checked the internet and made a list of the local fortune tellers. Okay, maybe I felt a bit guilty about breaking my promise to be the new Hand of Fate, but there was no point in pretending any more. Once I'd banished the backlog *djinns* and *djemons*, the whole Hand of Fate bit would be pretty much done with. Rhys could take care of the paranormal community; all I needed to do was to clear up the mess with Mimsy's djemon, find a temporary replacement for Charlie Crimmer, and find a fortune teller to take over my great-grandmother's clients. Then I could get back to my regularly scheduled life.

I walked the three blocks back to my apartment.

The front was still barricaded and covered with yellow tape, so I cut through the wooded lot behind my place. I paused in the woods for a minute, checking to make sure no one was around. The charred ruins of my landlady's house and garage looked awful. The place hadn't been much to look at before, but the nice tree out front had also been scorched, and the stark scene looked like something out of a nightmare. It also made me aware of how exposed the carriage house was. Without the house and tree and garage to shield it from the street, the carriage house stood out like a sore thumb.

I trotted across the strip of lawn to my back door and let myself in. The acrid smell of smoke and soot lingered in the air. Water lay in puddles on the floor, and the sound of dripping came from above me. I moved cautiously through the hallway toward the front. The front door was gone; the entrance had been boarded over. I tiptoed up the stairs and stared in dismay at the wreckage of my apartment.

The big front window in the living room was gone; as was about half of the roof above it. Broken glass littered the floor and the sofa was soaking wet. The floor-to-ceiling bookcase with my treasured collection of paperback romance novels had been toppled. The sofa cushions been tossed across the room and lay scattered like corpses across the squishy wet carpet.

The apartment had come furnished; the loss wasn't mine, but the whole place looked like a disaster area. I didn't have renters insurance and with my landlady in jail, I didn't think I'd have much luck getting the place livable anytime soon. It didn't matter that I'd been evicted; this place had been my home for four years. My black and white cats-eye clock had been pulled off the wall and crushed underfoot. *Oh man.*

Stepping carefully around the shards of glass, I took a quick peek at the kitchen. It was a disaster too, but the only fire damage appeared to be a thick layer of soot near the ceiling. There wasn't any water on the floor, but the firemen had swept everything out all the cupboards and even the drawers and oven, throwing everything onto the floor. What a mess. I found a barely crushed box of strawberry pop-tarts and headed back to my bedroom, munching on the broken pieces for breakfast.

Like the kitchen, my bedroom and bathroom had been trashed. Someone had pulled all my clothes out of my closet and dumped them on my bed. Everything in the drawers had been dumped on the floor and scattered. The reek of smoke infiltrated everything. Luckily, the flames hadn't come anywhere near this part of the apartment. I'd have to do laundry if I didn't want to smell like a campfire; but the water and power had been turned off. All I could do was to shove as many clothes as I could into my backpack and walk away.

When I opened the bedroom window to get some fresh air, the realization hit me. This mess hadn't been caused by the firemen, although the mess in my living room was easily explained. My apartment had been searched.

Thoroughly.

My heart fluttered uncomfortably. Someone had come in here after the firemen left. Other than the mess, I couldn't see that anything had been taken. Robbery made no sense—I had nothing worth stealing. It gave me the creeps, and I didn't want to stick around. I grabbed my boots and shouldered my backpack.

I crept back down the stairs and unlocked the door to my storage unit. This part of the building had been untouched, by both the fire fighters and whoever had searched my apartment.

I got a happy surprise when I opened the door. The contents hadn't been touched. Most of the stuff in here were things Lance hadn't had room for at his place. His racing motorcycles were in their usual spots, parked right next to mine. Whoever robbed me hadn't known about these bikes.

Lance had a Ducati 1098 Superbike and Kawasaki ZX-14; more than twenty thousand dollars worth of bikes. I sighed with relief. Wherever Lance was, he hadn't gone far. And if he'd been mad at me, he would never have left them here.

Whether he'd gone into rehab or not, I had to find him.

I put on my helmet and chaps and walked my

Victory Hammer S out to the driveway before locking up again. She's a heavy bike, and not exactly a looker; built low enough to the ground that I can plant both feet while astride. Lance helped me find her used a few years ago, and customized her for me as a birthday present. It's a good bike for a woman, at its best out on the open highway, so I rarely ride it around town unless I don't have a choice.

I swung my leg over she started up with purr. This was nothing like the motorized trikes we used at work. Even in idle, she gave me a thrill. For the first time in days. I started to feel like I was finally in control of *something*.

I eased the bike slowly down the driveway, and then goosed the gas when I got to the street. Something about the powerful rumble of an engine between my legs makes me feel invincible. By the time I reached Bayshore, I was ginning like fool.

Violet Langley, Lance's ex-wife, remarried a few years ago and now lives in Honeoye Falls, about twenty-five miles south of Shore Haven. It's a darling, well-preserved, rural village located at the far end of the county. The streets are quaint; most of the houses are either new or nearly two hundred years old. The Langleys lived in a newer, three-bedroom townhouse on a forested lot overlooking the creek. Until recently, Violet and Lance shared custody of their nine-year-old daughter, Mina.

Mina's screamed when she saw me at the door. She was in my arms in a flash; clinging to me like a monkey.

"Mattie! Where have you been?" She rubbed bunny noses with me and I put her down.

"Oh it hasn't been that long, sweetie."

"Hello, Mattie." Even Violet looked pleased to see me. Our relationship had warmed somewhat, even as her relationship with Lance had disintegrated. I'd finally stopped making excuses for him, and she'd stopped seeing me as an enabler. She and Lance had only been married for four years, but we'd known each other all our lives. "What brings you out this way?"

"I was hoping I could talk to you." I jerked my head toward Mina. "Privately?"

"What? Is it about my birthday?" asked Mina. Her dark eyes sparkled.

"No, Miss Nosey," I said. "And your birthday isn't for another month. This is big girl talk."

"That's right young lady. You're supposed to be picking up your room. Now Aunt Mattie and I are going to step outside for a few minutes, and when I get back, there better be nothing on the floor in there. No socks, no stuffed animals, no toys. Understand?"

The eye roll said it all. "Okay."

Violet barely waited until we'd gotten outside. "Have you heard from him?"

In her shaded front yard, trilliums bloomed beneath the trees. A catbird hopped in and out of the lilac bushes, pecking at bugs in the leaf litter.

"No. I haven't seen him since the funeral. I went to his house the other day, and he's gone. Completely moved out without telling me."

Violet is seven years older than me, but people who see us together sometimes think we're sisters. We both have long dark hair, an athletic build, and olive complexions. But Violet's got these expressive blue eyes that really tell you everything she's thinking. And I could tell she was worried before she said a word.

"He told me he was going back to rehab. He knows that's the only way he'll ever get to see Mina. I told him to let me know where he was going."

She pulled a card out of the pocket of her sweater. "The next day, this was in my mailbox. There's no postmark." She handed it to me.

It was a postcard with a picture of an Atlantic City casino on the front. On the back, the message said: *Having fun, wish you were here-- L*

"It's so weird. I don't know what to think." Tiny frown lines wrinkled her forehead. "Why would he do something like that? He's not a cruel man."

I ran my hand across the block-letter printing. It might have been Lance's, but somehow, I didn't believe it. "Lance has never written a postcard in his life. I can't believe he would have sent this one."

Her breath caught. "That's what I thought!"

I waved the card at her. "Can I keep this? I'm going to go look for him."

"Yes. Please, Mattie. And let me know what you find, okay? Mina keeps asking about him. She was too young to remember the last time he was in rehab, so I told her he's in a special school for a few weeks. Call me as soon as you know something."

I told her I would and headed back to Shore Haven.

There was a FOR RENT sign in the front window of Lance's house when I rode up. The landlords, Hal and Marie Mitchell, are a retired couple who live next door. Hal did not look happy to see me.

"Oh. Hullo Mattie."

A few weeks ago, I'd been baby-sitting Mina when a couple of thugs came by looking for Lance. Long story short, I'd lied to Hal and Marie about them, and they hadn't believed me.

"I was looking for Lance."

He gave me a wary look. "Packed up and moved a week ago. Just left a note in the mailbox. Told us to keep the security and cleaning deposit. Not even thirty days notice."

It sounded like an accusation. "Um, did he give you a forwarding address?"

"Nope."

He started to close the door. "Um, how much are you asking for the rent?" I know it was probably out of my price range, but I had to move anyway, and I had this wild idea that if I rented his place, maybe Lance would be able to find me.

He stared at me like I was mad. "No offense, but we're just as glad your brother's gone. Between the arrest and those goons you hang out with, we're not interested in renting to either of you." When he closed the door, I heard the deadbolt lock.

I tried Lance's cell phone again, and this time there was a recording saying that the line was out of service. There was only one other place to look.

CHAPTER 16

EXCEPT FOR A three-year period when Lance was heavily into gambling, Lance and Doc had been best friends since eighth grade and partners in the garage since just after high school. Their shop was in Pictson, just two blocks east of the Police Department and City Hall, so it was no surprise they'd eventually been contracted to service all the city vehicles. The Aapex Bike and Auto Shop didn't look like much from the outside; a six-bay enclosed garage refurbed from a 1960's era used-car dealership, with a chain-link fence around a parking lot that was usually filled to capacity with cars.

The reception area was a cramped little glass-walled room overlooking the parking lot, lined with orange plastic chairs, a coffee maker, a popcorn popper, and a big-assed television. Doc's wife, Glenna handled the customers and kept the coffee and popcorn machines humming.

But anyone privileged enough to set foot inside

said six-bay garage immediately knew they were in the presence of master mechanics. Not a speck of grease marred the floors or tools; even the trash cans were clean. The old showroom floor had been converted into the body and paint shop, and it too, had the same well-tended, almost shrine-like atmosphere.

The shop was closed on Sundays, but Doc and Glenna had converted the sales office on the second floor into their home. I buzzed the intercom at the front gate, and the electric gate slid open.

Like Lance, Doc is first and foremost a motorcycle guy. The two of them raced bikes on the local circuit until Doc had a bad crash and lost his leg; or most of it, anyway. Even with the prosthetic, he knew his racing days were over, and with the insurance money, he and Lance opened the shop.

"Your Honda is going to need a new transmission, Mattie. Not only that, but you got a blown piston. Probably going to need a ring job, too. And the undercarriage is about rusted through..."

Doc is grumpy guy. Always has been, always will be. It's just his nature, I guess. And when you add in the bald head and scraggly beard and tattoos; he's intimidating as hell. But underneath, he's really a big old softie. The whole time he was itemizing what was wrong with Trusty Rusty; his eyes were glued to my bike. The Victory Hammer S is designed for short men or women; at six-foot-six, Doc will never ride one, but he likes mine a lot.

"I know how much you like this car, but you'd be better off selling it for scrap and getting something else."

"Have you heard from Lance?"

"No. Are you listening? The car isn't safe to drive."

"Aren't you curious as to where he is?"

"I know where he is, and frankly, I don't care anymore. Whatever he want to do with his life is just fine by me."

"Where is he?"

Doc patted the pockets of his jean jacket. "Got it here somewhere. Here."

It was another postcard from Atlantic City.

Later - L.

"When did you get this?"

"Friday, I guess. Look Mattie. We both know what this means. I'm not going to waste my energy on his problems anymore. Frankly, I'm too busy tryin' to keep this place running. I was pissed as hell when he didn't show up for work all week, but after all the craziness been going on lately, I figured he needed a few days. That card is a slap in the face, as far as I'm concerned."

The card was exactly the same as Violet's. "Doc, he didn't send this. Look, there's no postmark."

Doc shook his head. "Don't kid yourself, Mattie.

The message is clear. He knows we're through if he goes down that road again. I just wish he'd had the balls to say it to my face."

"I think something's happened to him."

He gave me a sour look. "What do you want to do about your car?"

I didn't have the five thousand dollars it would cost to fix Rusty, and I had way too much on my mind to think about getting another car right away. Besides, I'd seen a Fortune Teller's sign on the way over here, and I wanted to check it out. So I asked Doc to hold onto Rusty for a few days, and took the postcard with me.

I'd probably driven past Miss Felicia's Psychic Cottage a thousand times without seeing it, but this time, the blue neon sign saying 'no appointment necessary' had my name written all over it. I parked my bike on the street out front and walked up the front walk, my heart yammering in my chest. I told myself that I was just there to introduce myself and find out what kind of place this was. I mean, the house was just a little place, nothing like Madame Coumlie's big painted lady. A modest, hand painted sign announced that hours were Wednesday through Sunday, 11-4pm, excepting holidays.

A sullen Goth girl of about twelve or thirteen answered my knock. Black boots, shredded skirt, chains, and black lipstick; the whole works.

"Um, I'm here to see Miss Felicia?"

She stuck out her hip. "It's ninety dollars for thirty minutes. You pay first."

"I'm not here for a reading. I just want to talk to Miss Felicia."

"Doesn't matter, lady. Its ninety bucks. What do you want to talk to her about?"

"I don't--. It's a business matter. Really. Could you please just tell her I'd like to talk to her?"

From somewhere in the back of the house, a woman's voice rang out. "Who is it, Val?"

"Some woman. She doesn't want to pay."

"No, it's not that. I--." I checked my wallet. No way I had ninety dollars on me. I held up three crumpled twenties. "This is all I've got." I shouted to the unseen woman at the back of the house. "I'm not here for a reading; I just want to talk to you!"

Goth girl Val snatched the twenties out of my hand. "This will buy you fifteen minutes. Follow me."

Geeze.

Val escorted me into a snug living room and told me to take a seat before slouching out to get her mother. A heavy flagstone fireplace dominated one wall, but windows on three sides kept the room bright and airy. A couple of caramel-colored corduroy recliners faced each other over a low table. On one wall hung a large, framed, brightly-colored mandala over a trickling indoor fountain. Potted plants sat on every surface except the reading table.

A few moments later, Miss Felicia entered the room; a questioning expression on her face. Blonde, blue-eyed, and in her late thirties, she looked tanned and fit, especially in the tennis whites she was wearing. Not exactly my idea of a fortune teller. She had a peaceful serenity about her. I liked her right away.

"I'm sorry, I really can't do a proper reading in less than thirty minutes."

No, I'm not here for a reading. I just wanted to talk to you--."

She took my hand, her grip firm.

"Oh." Her eyes went wide. "Well look at all those spirits." She dropped my hand like she'd been burned. "You're the Hand of Fate!"

Dang, she was good. "Well, sort of. She was my great-grandmother."

"I knew her. I mean, I met her a few times." She wiped her hand on her skirt. "But—she was nothing like you. What do you want?"

"Her clients are upset; they want me to help them, and I can't. I don't have the gift."

She motioned me to sit in one of the recliners. "Of course you can. *You're the Hand of Fate.*"

"I mean I don't have the sight. Like just now, when you walked into the room and said those things; I mean, there is no way you would have known that. I can't do that. And believe me; I've even been tested by the FBI. I got zippo on the old psychic detection test."

"Take off those contact lenses you're wearing. You'd be surprised at how different the world looks."

Without contact lenses, my eyes are the same faded copper color as my great-grandmothers. Off-putting to most, freakish to others, including myself. Wearing the colored contacts gives me a reflection in the mirror I recognize. "Why I'm trying to say, is that I'd like you to take over Madame Coumlie's clients. I don't know anything about telling fortunes, and I've already got a job." She sat back in her chair, and I knew I'd somehow insulted her. "I mean, I work for the City."

"I see. You mean that handing out parking tickets is more real, more *important*, than sharing your gift with people who really need you. Isn't that right?"

"I hate to keep turning these people away. To be honest, I didn't ask to be the Hand of Fate. I don't mind banishing a few *djemons*, but I don't want any of the rest of it. I want my old life back."

She stiffened and stood. "Your power rolls off you in waves; so strong I can hardly breathe, and you tell me you won't use it to help people? You control legions of the undead; *djemons*, *djenies*, *djinn*. Any one of them is a slave to your commands. You're surrounded by restless souls, begging you to help them find peace. You're the queen of the dead. The living incarnation of chaos!"

She was shouting now. "You've got the power, *use it!* I don't know what kind of game you're playing, but you've already wasted quite enough of my time. Get the hell out of my house."

Sheesh. If I'd had a tail, I'd have tucked it between my legs.

As soon as I got back to Henri's, I went down to the basement to wash the smoky clothes I'd managed to take from my apartment. Henri followed me down; he must have known there was something wrong. I told him about my unsuccessful search for Lance.

But it was more than Lance's disappearance that had me stewing. Miss Felicia's comments on my powers had unnerved me. If I did have some kind of psychic powers, maybe I could use them to find Lance. And then there was that other bit; the part about being able to command the undead.

"Tell me, Henri. What are you planning to do with your life?"

He looked surprised. "I want to experience this physical plane. See the world, as you would say. "

I stuffed a load of whites into the washing machine and added detergent. Not my brand, but beggars couldn't be choosey. "What if I asked you to stay?"

"I would of course acquiesce to your wishes."

"Why? I'm not your master. You owe me no loyalty."

Henri paused for a moment, as if choosing his words. "When a *djemon's* master dies, and he is transformed into a *djenie*, the compulsion to obey does not leave entirely. I cannot speak for others, but as a new djenie, I am often fearful. Rhys says that fear gradually recedes, and with it, much of the compulsion to seek out a new human master."

"So if I wanted you to stay and take over Madame Coumlie's clients you would do it? Not that I'm asking, mind you. But I spoke to a psychic today about taking over Madame's clients. She suggested that I had power over all the undead, including *djenies*. Anything I wanted, they'd do it."

Henri sighed. "The human myth of *djenies* is that they must always obey their master's wishes. But of course, the djenie cannot exist before the master dies; thus no *djenie* ever has a human master."

"Thank goodness it's not true, then."

Henri stared at me with a look of such longing and yearning, I took a step back. "What?"

"You truly are the Hand of Fate, Mattie. Your powers far eclipse your great-grandmother's."

"So what?"

"Madame told me you were the result of three generations of inbreeding. Before she married Dirk Coumlie, Madame gave birth to Otto Russ's son Werner, out of wedlock. Werner was taken from her and adopted by Otto and his wife. Several years later, Madame and Dirk had a daughter, Oleanna. Oleanna and Werner fell in love and Oleanna's mother died giving birth to your mother, Olivia. Werner's son, Garlan Russ, was your father. This is why you are so powerful. Your approval is like a drug to me and all those like me. I would do anything you asked. Anything."

I slid down the washing machine to the floor. I knew it had to be something like that. I closed my eyes. *I really am a monster.*

Henri squatted beside me. "I didn't mean to cause you pain, Mattie. But you cannot understand how powerful your grip is on my kind. We are attracted to you like a moth to a flame. We love you. We would willingly die for you. "He took my hands in his. "We cannot help ourselves. Although *djenies* serve no master; we have no free will before you, our queen."

The weight of his words burned into me. *We have no free will before you.* No one should have that much power. If Henri was right, Rhys's feelings for me meant nothing. He couldn't help himself. It wasn't real.

And it never had been.

CHAPTER 17

I DIDN'T HEAR from Lance that night. Or Rhys either.

I called Agent Frank Porter, with the Rochester branch of the FBI; but he wasn't there *either*, so I left him a message. I asked to call me, saying my brother Lance had been missing for three days at least. Maybe I should have called Sheriff Reynolds first, but he wasn't fond of either me or Lance. Frank Porter respected me; it made more sense to call someone who didn't think I wasn't a nutjob.

I still hadn't decided what to do about Rhys. If Henri was right, and *djenies* had no free will around me, then keeping both of them out of my life was the best thing for everyone involved. So the sooner I could finangle my way out of this whole Hand of Fate scenario, the better.

The one bright spot of my day was the Lacey Lippmann interview. Mayor Brunson wanted an interview for the employee newspaper. I'd been dreading it all morning.

But it went great. Mayor Brunson was there, along with my boss, Mike Olsen. There was a little ceremony afterword in the employee coffee room. There was a cake, and the mayor presented me with a plaque, the 'Breath of Life' award, while a photographer took our picture. For the interview, Lacey was on her best behavior, with hardly a smirk, even though I could see it about killed her to be civil.

After the ceremony, people asked the mayor about the layoff rumors; but as expected, he wouldn't say much. For once, I was glad I'd gotten attention for doing something good. For now, at least, I was pretty sure that being in the Mayor's good graces probably didn't hurt my chances of keeping my job.

At the end of my shift, I found Agent Porter waiting for me in an unmarked government vehicle in the parking lot. He had somebody with him.

"What are *you* doing here?"

Porter is a big man; not fat, but beefy. Barrel-chested. He wears western-cut suits and cowboy boots that probably drive his pals at the bureau batty, but he doesn't care. He's from Texas, and that's just the way they are, I guess.

"I wanted to introduce you to my replacement. This is Ted Roper."

Except for the auburn hair and freckles, Roper looked every bit as humorless and by-the-book as any other law enforcement officer I'd ever met. White starched shirt. Hair trimmed so short you could see the shape of his skull. Something about him put me immediately on the defensive. Of course, I'd thought the same thing about Porter, when I first met him, but this guy stared at me with a coldness that gave me shivers. His hand, when I shook it, was hard and bony.

"And that's Jager."

Porter jerked his head toward the black dog sitting in the back seat.

A *djenie* dog. Like Luhng.

I pulled my hand back from Roper like I'd been burned. Good heavens, the FBI was using a *djenie* dog to find unlicensed demon masters! I wondered if Roper knew what he had. Even knowing that Blix and Larry were nowhere near, I broke into a cold sweat.

"Ted and Jager are working with the arson inspector on the fire at your landlady's house."

I struggled to keep my voice calm. "Why is the FBI involved in a house fire?"

"Your landlady is under arrest as a suspected demon master. That's a federal beef, and that fire was not accidental. We just came from there. Jager alerted in several places, including the source of the blaze. He's been trained to alert at the scent of demons."

Roper's gentle voice was at odds with his unapproachable appearance. He reached into the open window of the car and the *djemon* dog fawned beneath his hand, just like any real dog would.

"We'd like your permission to bring him into your place as well."

My heart skipped a beat. "You think I had something to do with the fire?"

"Not at all. Just routine."

"Fine. I'll follow you over there."

I was so preoccupied with the dog, I nearly rear-ended their car at a stoplight. I had no doubt that Jager would find traces of Blix and Larry in my apartment. I had to think of something, and fast.

I couldn't very well claim that Patty's demon had been hanging out in my apartment. I couldn't claim innocence, especially since Porter knew that Rhys and I had banished the *djinn* from the government-secured cavern beneath Sentinel Hill. I needed to do something about that dog.

I remembered what Henri and Miss Felicia had told me. As the Hand of Fate, I had dominion over the dead. Or the non-living, at any rate.

I was about to find out if they were right. I whipped the bike around them in the afternoon traffic and beat them to my apartment.

With the driveway still blocked off by yellow tape, I waited for them out front. Jager leapt out of the car as soon as Roper gave the word; seemingly eager to get to work. If this was going to work, this would be my only chance.

"Can I pet him?"

Roper seemed just as eager to get to work as his dog, but reluctantly allowed me to approach.

Jager looked like a black German Shepherd, with ears that pricked forward, a pointy nose and lots of sharp teeth. Like all the other *djenies* I'd met, he had golden eyes, which really popped against his black fur.

I extended the back of my closed fist for him to sniff. "Nice doggie."

He took a whiff and threw himself to the ground, rolled over and presented his tummy to be rubbed. I caught a disgusted look on Roper's face, but ignored it. "Good boy," I gave his belly a brief scratch. "You'll *never* smell anything interesting on me or any of *my* stuff." I sort of *pushed* my will into him. Our eyes met, and I got the feeling he understood.

Roper wanted Jager to search my apartment with as few distractions as possible, so Porter and I waited outside while they searched. I was so nervous I could barely stand, but I forced myself to make chit-chat with Porter while they were inside. I asked him about Lance and he told me he couldn't get involved until the local authorities made an official request.

"I spoke with Sheriff Reynolds personally, and he assured me he was taking your missing persons report seriously. That's all I can do. This isn't the first time your brother's gone missing. I'm sure he'll turn up when he's good and ready."

Almost exactly what they'd told me when I filled out the missing persons report. If I was going to find Lance, I was going to have to do it myself. I asked Porter when he was leaving.

"End of the month. It's just a temporary assignment, for now. Agent Roper and I are trading assignments for six months. It works out great. New Orleans is less than a six-hour drive from Houston, so I'll be spending the holidays with my folks this winter, while Roper's shoveling three feet of snow off his sidewalk in minus thirty wind chills."

"He doesn't sound like he's from the south."

Porter shook his head. "Nope, Montana. We were in the same class at the academy."

"Seems like a real hard-nose."

"We just have a different way of doing things. Once you get to know him--."

"I can't see him and Rhys getting along."

Porter made a face. "Yeah, well you're probably right about that. Maybe it's for the best."

As jumpy as I was already feeling, my stomach took a bad turn. "What's for the best?"

"Rhys is going back to Scotland."

I froze.

Roper and Jager came down the driveway toward us. I could tell from Roper's expression that they'd found nothing. Jager was pulling on the leash to get to me for another belly rub.

"*Scotland?* When did he tell you this?"

"I thought you knew. He's leaving at the end of the month."

Jager, much to Roper's embarrassment, groveled at my feet for another belly rub. "It's clean. Let's go."

"You sound disappointed." I tickled Jager's tummy while he squirmed delightedly. *Good Boy.*

"I wanted this assignment because Shore Haven is supposed to be this big hotspot for demons. But so far, we've turned up squat. After New Orleans, this is a bit of a letdown." He opened the back door of their car and motioned to Jager. With a seemingly apologetic look for me, the *djenie* dog leapt in, his tongue lolling happily to one side.

I watched them drive away, my mood as black as Jager's fur. I didn't want Rhys to leave. My mind swirled with confusion. I didn't believe he didn't have something going on with *Savanne*; certainly not after I'd seen her pawing him. But at the same time, I couldn't discount what Henri had said, or my own feelings. *What the hell is going on with Rhys?* I needed to talk to him. Alone. But if I did, I was afraid I'd ask him not to leave. And if I did that, based on what Henri had said and what I'd just seen from Jager, he'd stay. Because I wanted him to, and *only* because I wanted him to. Because he had no choice but to obey.

CHAPTER 18

THE NEXT MORNING, my route had me in downtown Shore Haven; which was pretty cool, because everyone had seen me on the news, and wanted to congratulate me.

I felt pretty good. So good, that when I was heading back to Picston at the end of my shift, and saw a woman dressed in a very short pirate costume pulled over by the side of the road, crying her eyes out, I pulled over to see what the problem was. Mattie the hero to the rescue.

"It ran right out in front of me," she sobbed. "I didn't have time to stop. I *know* I hit it, I felt the wheels roll over it. But now I can't find it, and I'm late for work." She peered into the deep grass growing along the roadside.

She told me she worked at the Captain's Club, a lakeside tavern in Webster. That explained the maroon skirt and ruffled panties with the black corset big gold earrings. The four-inch spike heels kept her from stepping off the road; she was afraid she'd ruin her shoes in the mud. I don't think she realized that with an outfit that skimpy, no one would ever notice her shoes.

"It's a little black kitten. He should be right here."

I had no problem wading into the knee-high grass. Usually the groundhogs do a pretty good job of keeping the grass along the roadsides short, but for some reason, the culvert here was overgrown. I used my hands to part the grass. It didn't' take me long to find it.

That was no kitten. It was a very small djenie. And it was in very bad shape.

The cocktail waitress gave me a cardboard shoebox from the back of her car to carry the wounded *djenie* in. I couldn't just leave it there, I had to do something. The nearest vet clinic was in Shore Haven, so I turned the trike around and headed back.

The sign outside the Shore Haven Veterinary Clinic said they specialized in exotics, so I planned to just drop it off. But when I entered the clinic, the vet, Dr. Jensen was standing in the reception area, talking to his receptionist. As soon as I showed him the wounded *djenie*, he agreed to see us right away.

He must've known what it was; he didn't even bat an eye. I followed him back into a tiny, windowless examination room and set the box on top of the metal examination table. The room smelled faintly of antiseptic, but the soft yellow walls, adorned with cute pictures of cats and a poster about Lyme disease kept the room from being entirely sterile.

"It was hit by a car. Run over, actually."

He gently lifted out the poor creature out of the box. There was no blood, but it was so badly mangled, I couldn't make head or tail out of its form until he laid it out on the table.

My heart fluttered. A pterodactyl. Just like Annie. A little moan escaped my throat.

Was it Annie? *No.* Couldn't be. If it was, then that meant Mimsy... *No.*

"Do you know what this is?" His eyes drifted to my nametag. "Officer Blackman."

"Yes." I nodded. "Will you put it down?"

"I can't. They're immune to all our drugs." He sounded regretful. "You're the new Hand of Fate, aren't you?"

I frowned. "You know, I lived my whole life in this town, and never heard of the Hand of Fate. Now I hear it everywhere I go."

He grinned. "That's nothing. I specialize in dogs and cats. Yet at least twice a week I get a call from the zoo or I'm talking about road kill with some Good Samaritan, telling them there's nothing I can do *because these things aren't animals.*"

He was cute. Dimples, nice teeth, the whole bit;

right down to the wedding ring. "Touché."

He put the limp djenie back in the shoebox. "I'll tell you what I told Madame Coumlie. Take it home. Put it in the basement with the others. It'll recover or it won't."

"That's it?"

"Super-naturals are more your area of expertise than mine, Officer Blackman."

If he wasn't so cute, I would have slapped him.

CHAPTER 19

ON MY WAY home, I swung by Mystic Properties, and noticed Rhys' big black pickup parked out back. Okay, maybe I'd been sort of cruising by every time I got a chance, but I wanted to catch him alone for once. A private conversation. I wanted to ask him--. Well, I wasn't sure what I wanted. Closure, maybe. I still couldn't understand if what I thought we felt for each other was true or, if Henri was right, just a Hand of Fate thing.

I parked my city scooter next to his truck. The back door was wide open, so I took off my helmet and shook out my hair, then tucked the shoebox underneath my arm and stepped inside.

I stood in the doorway a moment, letting my eyes adjust to the dim interior. Rhys was seated on the old overstuffed grey sofa, grading papers. He had them stacked all over the coffee table in front of him. When he saw me, a grin lit up is face and he rose, rubbing his hands on the front of his black jeans.

He looked good.

He came toward me, silent and deliberate as a panther on the prowl. The bite marks were gone. That thought alone gave me pause. Suddenly, I seemed to forget everything I'd wanted to say. Instead, I swallowed hard and shoved the shoebox at him.

"It's a hurt *djenie*. I took it to the vet, but there's nothing he can do."

His grin paled a bit, but he took the box and set it on the coffee table without even looking at it. "Nice to see you too Mattie."

His eyes never left my face.

"I don't' know what to do with it. I figured since you're the djenie social services department, you might want it."

"What's the matter?"

Even though I knew he was wearing contact lenses, those green eyes of his had me feeling weak in the knees. The room was warm, but every few seconds the big oscillating fan in the corner swept over me, almost as if it was beckoning me further into the room.

"Porter says you're leaving." I blurted the words before I knew what I was saying.

He pressed his lips together. "Madame Coumlie asked me to come to Shore Haven before she knew about you. She was dying, and needed someone to take over for her. Not as the Hand of Fate; her role in the anomalous community here was more of an honorific. She wanted someone to continue her role as the guardian of this place. She was the very soul of Shore Haven, Mattie. And now it's your turn. There's no reason for me to stick around."

"But I don't want the job! I never wanted it. At first I thought it was kind of cool to be able to banish djinn and help people, but this isn't the life I wanted. I already have a job, Rhys. The whole Hand of Fate thing is out of control. Everywhere I go, people want--. I can't help these people. You can. They need you. Please--." I clapped my hand over my mouth to stop myself before I said the words. *Please stay.*

"This is your destiny, Mattie, not mine."

This was not going the way I wanted. I wanted him to *want* to stay. Because he wanted to. Because of his feelings for me, Mattie-the-meter-maid. Not because Mattie the Hand of Fate asked him to. Not the same thing.

"You said you liked it here."

"I do. Shore Haven is everything Madame Coumlie told me it would be. And more." His eyes met mine. "Things have gotten pretty complicated."

Little fluttery sensations crept up my inner thighs. I could feel the heat radiating off his body. He wanted me too, I was certain. If he reached for me, I would be helpless. But I just couldn't bring myself to make the first move.

"What about Henri? And all the others you'll be

leaving behind?"

"Is that really why you're here? To talk about Henri?"

My body felt so tight I thought I'd scream. "No, I--."

He pulled me to him. The sensation was like being enveloped in a furnace. He didn't just wrap his arms around me, he drew me into his heat and held me there until all my confusion and resistance melted away and there was only his lips and hands and the melding of minds and bodies.

I don't know how long he kissed me. It felt like an eternity.

It felt like a fraction of a second.

When he stepped back, we both gasped for breath.

"I don't want to be the Hand of Fate!"

He touched his fingers to his lips. "When I kiss you, I feel... things I haven't felt in so long, I've forgotten them. I would die for you Mattie. *Tell me* what you want from me."

I bit my lips together so hard they hurt. Wasn't he *asking* me to tell him to stay? *I couldn't do that. I wouldn't do that.* I shook my head, and the moment passed. "What if I wasn't the Hand of Fate? Would you stay or go?"

He kissed my forehead. "You can't change your fate, girl. It is what it is."

It was over. We both knew it. Over before it ever really got started.

"What am I supposed to do about this little *djenie*?"

"Order it to live."

CHAPTER 20

I RODE OVER to Henri's house with the wounded *djenie*. I felt as bruised and battered as the poor little pterodactyl. Rhys wanted me to order him to stay, and I wanted him to stay without being ordered to by the Hand of Fate. My skin still burned from where he'd touched me, and I wanted him more than anything I could imagine. *Never gonna happen.*

Fine. From now on, I'd just plain old Mattie Blackman, thank you very much. All I had to do was to rid myself of everything related to the Hand of Fate.

I carried the box down to the cool basement, glad that Henri wasn't home, for once. I didn't feel like talking to anyone. I grabbed a clean, still-warm towel from the dryer and wrapped it around the wounded pterodactyl *djenie*. She made a small mewling noise, but quieted down right away.

"Now you hear me, little *djenie*. I am ordering you to get better, hear me?"

One eye opened briefly, and I glimpsed the tell-tale

golden pupil.

"You're safe here, little one." Suddenly, I remembered the other denizens living in the darker corners of the basement. "And the rest of you are not to harm her, understand? That's an order, too."

I heard the doorbell ring upstairs. I thought about ignoring it, but I still needed to get the trike back to Picston and clock out for the day anyway. Probably someone else looking to get their fortune read. I really needed to get Henri to take that big sign down.

Unlike the others who'd come to the door, this bandy-legged little fellow sported a wide grin as cheery as a Buddha. The first thing I noticed about him was his multicolored lifeline; something I'd never seen before.

"You have a few minutes, Miz Blackman?" He was brown-skinned, and balding, with even white teeth and an ageless face. He could have been anywhere between forty to eighty years old.

"I was just leaving."

"Clarence Shango at your service, ma'am." He offered me his card. "I was a friend of Miz Coumlie's. I'm sorry for your loss. I had me a little *bidness* deal I was workin' with her before she died. Only take a minute of your time."

His accent carried a bit of the islands as well as the South. I glanced at the card. Clarence Shango, on Lamarque Street in Algiers Louisiana. Strange names. Never heard of the place. "What kind of business?"

"Pest control." Shango's smile was contagious. "I'm surprised she didn't mention it to you. I'm a licensed *djemon* exterminator."

My heart skipped a beat. This was the answer to all my problems. Or a big bunch of them, at any rate.

"Come in." I grinned and showed him into the parlor.

Shango explained that after hurricane Katrina, his 'bidness' had fallen off, nearly to nothing. "I kept tryin' to make a go of it, but it was no good any more. When I decided to look 'round for a new place to set up shop, Shore Haven was my first choice."

In some circles, Shore Haven is known as the spirit capital of the Northeast. Maybe not quite as much charisma as New Orleans or Santa Fe, but the reputation is fairly earned.

"I met with Miz Coumlie some time back and she agreed to let me take over the demon work, seein' as she's getting on, you see. But then she died, before we had a chance to work out the details and transfer her clients. I am hoping to open a place here in town." He winked at me. "Now I hear how you just 'bout cleared the whole town of a whole lotta the strays, so mebbe you don' need ol' Papa Shango anymore."

"No! That's not it at all." I liked him and didn't want to lose him. Shore Haven needed Shango. "We need you more than you can possibly know. Both the other exterminators in town shut down, so I'm all there is. I work full-time, and this is more than I can handle."

He grinned broadly at me. He seemed to be just about the liveliest man I'd ever met. His hands were gnarled and calloused, but the smooth skin of his face seemed untroubled by a single line. I couldn't help but wonder about the brilliant glow of his life line. Multiple strands of yellow, red, blue and purple.

"What method do you use?"

He shot me a startled look. "Say what?"

Blushing, I shifted in my seat. "To banish them."

He nodded wisely. "I do not banish demons, nor would I, even if I could. A demon's spirit is anchored to its master's soul like a barbed hook. I get 'em gone, and they don't come back."

I squirmed uncomfortably. "Then how do you get rid of them?'

He shook his finger at me. "Ah, that a little secret is what makes Papa Shango the best! My juju ain't so quick, but the soul ain't damaged and the demon don't nevah come back."

I felt a huge surge of warmth and gratitude for this man. There was definitely something special about him. "Where's your shop?"

"I'm still looking for the right location. My number is on the card. I can be reached there at any time, day or night. I'd be happy to take care of any referrals."

It was a local number.

This was a big load off my mind. With Shango to

take care of all the banishing, I could probably come up with a list of local fortune tellers for her other client referrals, and finally start concentrating on normal stuff, like getting my car fixed and finding a new place to live. And finding Lance. And Mimsy. *Ugh*, Mimsy.

And forgetting about Rhys. *Oh Rhys*. And getting back to my job. My *real* job. I wanted my old life back, and this guy had just offered to take over for me. About time things started going my way.

"This is great." I waved the card.

The phone in Madame Coumlie's kitchen started ringing. I told Shango I'd start sending him all the *bidness* he could handle, and sent him on his way.

The phone stopped ringing just as reached for it. Probably wasn't important. I put Shango's card next to the phone and headed out the door. I still had to drop the trike off back at work.

The phone started ringing again, and this time I answered it.

It was Mimsy's mother. Miriam was missing, and she seemed to think it was my fault.

I slid into a chair at the kitchen table and explained to her about Mimsy taking off while we'd been talking to Leung, but that only made Mrs. Wu start crying.

"I get a postcard from her today. She say she's not coming home."

A chill crept up my spine. "What kind of postcard? What does it say?" There was a pile of mail stacked up on the kitchen table. Bills and ads, mostly.

"Picture of New York Skyline. It says, *Don't wait up, Ma*. That's all. No postmark, no stamp."

Too many coincidences. The weirdest feeling or certainty came over me. I scattered the pile of mail, and sure enough, there it was. A picture postcard from Atlantic City. No stamp, no message, no signature.

"Luhng say she's dead."

I couldn't ignore the little voice in my head anymore. *What if that broken little pterodactyl in the basement was really Annie?* The blank postcard stared at me with an accusation. Mimsy couldn't be dead. One postcard didn't mean anything. But what about all those postcards from Lance?

No! I slammed my fist down on the table. "Look Mrs. Wu, I suggest you call the police and file a missing persons report on her. I don't know why Luhng would say that, but I'll go talk to him."

CHAPTER 21

I NEVER THOUGHT that dragons were capable of much expression, but I could tell that Luhng believed Mimsy was dead, even before he told me. The fierceness was still there, but the force of his personality was gone; as if the coals of his life force were no longer burning hot. Even his voice lacked the power he'd shown me previously.

He glared at me from beneath his heavy silver brow. "You are responsible." His heart didn't seem to be in it. "You are the harbinger of death. Everything you touch is poison. I blame you."

He held Larry in one arm, and seemed to take comfort from the little djragon's presence.

"What makes you so convinced she's dead?" But I knew he was right, even as I asked the question. I'd gone down into the basement before I left and the pterodactyl djenie reached her claw out to me. She knew me. I had no doubt it was Annie.

"She came to me. After you chased her away that

day, she returned. There was someone with her. A tall creature with ebony skin. She had some sort of power over Miriam."

My heart skipped a beat. *Savanne!*

"She wanted me to come with them. I refused, and demanded she release my namesake, but she laughed, and said Miriam belonged to her now."

"Maybe she's not dead. I think I know that woman. If I could talk to her. If there's something going on--."

"Miriam had no heartbeat. She did not breathe. She was nothing more than walking flesh. You've brought this evil into my clan. You must stop it."

He seemed so dispirited. "This is not my fault, Luhng. There's something going over at that club." I pointed toward the big house with the curtained windows, which stood facing us from the other side of Bayshore Drive. "Mimsy was already involved in it before I even knew her. But I promise you," I winced, even as I could not stop myself from saying the words. "I will find out what's going on over there, and if I can, I'll try to find Mimsy."

By the time I got the parking scooter back to its parking spot at Picston City Hall, it was after six o'clock and only a few folks remained in the building. My thoughts had been churning ever since I'd gotten that call from Mimsy's mother. The postcards somehow connected Mimsy's disappearance to Lance but I couldn't see how.

As I walked over to the employee parking lot to my bike, I spotted Lou Scali getting into his white Subaru station wagon. I'd gotten the feeling he knew more about the situation than he was willing to say in front of his partner. And Lou was one of us. Or at least, one of *them*; an anomalous individual. He had no lifeline. Whatever he was, Lou Scali wasn't human.

"Wait up, Lou!"

He gave me a double-take and I could see he didn't really want to talk to me. I sprinted over there before he could change his mind.

"Hey Mattie. I heard about your award, Congratulations."

"Thanks. There's something going on in that house down on Bayshore Drive. Mimsy, um Miriam Wu, that girl I was with when you found me the other day has gone missing. She hasn't been home since that day, and her mother found a postcard in their mailbox supposedly from her, saying she wasn't coming back."

"What do you want from me? You know the drill. If she's really missing, her parents ought to file a missing persons report. There's nothing I can do."

"I think she might be dead."

Lou glanced around the parking lot, before giving me a sharp look. "Why are you telling me?"

There was no one close enough to hear us. "I'm the

Hand of Fate, Lou. I can see things most people can't. And I can see you're not human."

His face paled.

"Mimsy went into that house, and now her djemon is dying. That can't happen if her master is alive."

"You should be careful about throwing around those kinds of allegations, Mattie. People can get hurt. People who have never done one thing against you."

"Oh come on, Lou, this is just you and me. The girl who used to bug you with all those questions about what it was like bein' a cop, remember? I'm not human anymore either. We're both members of the same club."

His shoulders relaxed a bit; he shook his head. "A dying demon isn't proof of anything."

"Yeah, but look at this." I pulled the postcard from Lance out of my pocket. "I just got the same kind of postcard from Lance. And he's missing, too. It's too big of a coincidence. There's gotta be something going on in that house."

He put his hand on my shoulder. "Look, I talked to Miriam Wu myself that day. She seemed perfectly normal; and made it clear that she did not want to leave. Her family is trying to coerce her into an arranged marriage, and said you were helping them. You were the one acting odd that day, remember? And as for your brother," he shrugged. "It's not the first time, is it? That postcard doesn't tie him to Miss Wu or that house."

Why couldn't he see it? "But you know something."

I could feel it like I knew my name. "There *is* something going on in that house. Both Mimsy and Lance are missing. Both their families have gotten postcards. How can that not mean something?"

"Mattie you're getting wound up over nothing. Yes, there have been a few complaints about the goings on over there. Noise, mostly. But don't push it. I didn't want to say anything, but Mrs. Sinaloa and her brother wanted to file a restraining order against you."

I stared at Lou. "*What?*"

"They were pretty hot for it, too. I asked them to wait twenty-four hours to let things cool down. They may go ahead anyway, but I would steer clear of that end of Bayshore Drive for the next few weeks, if I were you."

I was on my own.

CHAPTER 22

AT NOON THE next day, I stopped in at the Tax Assessor's office at City Hall and looked up the tax records on the house on Bayshore. I wanted to know who owned it. I needed a name.

I found a lot more than I expected. Blueprints, title transfer information, and the name of the owner, a Dr. Charles Williams, of New Orleans, Louisiana, who died in 1992. The house was now held by a private corporation called THE SINALOA FOUNDATION, LLC. The woman's name was Savanne Sinaloa. I stared at the local contact information. The property, now a rental, was managed by Mystic Properties; which in turn was *owned and operated by Rhys Warrick.*

The sight of Rhys's truck parked in Henri's driveway had me steaming, even before I parked the bike. Rhys had known who she was all along. He *had* to know what was going on at Club Lapis. All that nonsense about not remembering what happened that night had been a lie. If anything happened to Lance or Mimsy... The words of the psychic Felicia came back to me. *You've got the power, use it!*

I had the power to command Rhys to do my bidding. If he'd lied to me before, it was because I hadn't demanded the truth from him. Now I was going to make damn sure I got it.

With shaking hands, I popped out my colored contact lenses and put them in their little plastic carrying case. My eyes watered a little, I still wasn't completely used to them yet, but with a few quick blinks I felt better. Nothing would stand between me and the truth I needed from Rhys.

They were waiting for me in the parlor. Henri looked nervous; Rhys' expression was unreadable to me. The contact lenses he wore might fool some, but not me.

Not anymore.

"Mattie, we need to talk to you about this," Henri began. He waved Shango's business card at me.

"Let's start with the truth." I was too wound up to sit. I paced the floor, nearly rigid with righteousness. "I want the truth, Rhys. All of it. No, I don't just want it, I *demand* it. *As the Hand of Fate I command it.*"

Henri's eyes went wide.

Rhys's face hardened. "What are you talking about?"

"I'm talking about the Sinaloa Foundation. Ring

any bells? Mystic Properties manages the Club Lapis property, Rhys. You said someone was targeting people in the anomalous community. It looks to me like you're right in the middle of it."

Adrenalin surged through me. I was on a roll now; the fuse of my pent-up frustration had been lit, and I was in full-blown bitch mode.

"You've been renting that place to your 'missing' friend Savanne Sinaloa. That's right, the woman I saw you with at Club Lapis, the one you claim you can't remember, AKA Savanne Williams. She's not missing. She never was. You've been covering for her. You lied to me. About everything." My voice caught up in my throat. "And now she's got Lance and Mimsy, and maybe some of the others, too. So why don't you tell me what's going on?"

Angrily, I wiped the hot tears from my cheeks.

"Mattie, where did you get this?" Henri held Shango's card out to me.

"I don't care about that! I want answers, Rhys."

"Sit down, Mattie." Rhys' tone sounded dangerous. His eyes glittered with anger. "Please."

I slid into the rocking chair without a word.

"This is important. When did you speak to Shango?"

"Earlier today. What do you know about The Sinaloa Foundation?"

"If he's back, we're in big trouble." Henri said.

"I've got a hunch he never left," answered Rhys.

"Will one of you please tell me what's going on? What's the matter with Shango?" I remembered his multi-colored life line. "What is he?"

"He's human, or at least, he used to be. I don't know what he is, now," Henri said. "He came up here a few years ago, from New Orleans. He requested an interview with Madame Coumlie, and she agreed to see him. He arrived with a woman; a dead woman. A dead woman that he had reanimated by using her own *djemon*." Henri paused to let his words sink in.

"That's not possible." I looked at Rhys for confirmation. "Is it?"

"I've heard of it, but never seen it. Shango claimed to be an ninety-year-old psychic from Oklahoma who fled the dust bowl and worked his way through the carnival circuit during the depression. He presented himself as a psychic, admitted that in his youth, he'd made his living as a huckster and a small time con. He told us that while he was in Florida one winter, he met another carny who had been injured. The man was an alcoholic who made his own hooch from herbs and the rotted wood of poisonous shrubs. He claimed the resulting liquor was as strong as Everclear, and called it blue absinthe. The old man had back problems and a broken collar bone; he needed help running the still, so Shango agreed to help him out. The two men got to know one another, and got along well. One night, the old man confessed that he was a demon master. When

Shango doubted the story, he produced the *djemon*; introducing it by the name of Louis. Shango told us he was impressed, and persuaded the old man to agree to let him question the *djemon* in exchange for running the still and keeping him supplied with the absinthe."

"Can *djemons* talk?" I asked.

Henri nodded. "Of course. All djemons are able to answer direct question from their master; and if given permission or direction to do so, are able to speak to others."

I made a mental note to start talking to Blix. "I wish I'd known that earlier." I thought of Larry and wished I'd asked his feelings about being told to stay with Luhng. I already had a million questions I wanted to ask them, but now was not the time. "Go on."

"Shango told us that the old man was dying of alcoholic consumption; and his *djemon* was very small. It was not large enough to transition into a human form when his master passed. The creature, Louis, was in the form of a small serpent. It would be trapped in its snake shape, and after his masters death would mostly likely die. He asked the *djemon* if he would like to survive his master's passing and be willing to continue to serve and grow as Shango's *djemon*. Shango wasn't sure he could to it, but he had an idea he wanted to try, and felt he needed the *djemon's* cooperation. Louis, agreed, and Shango moved forward with his experiments.

"Shango said he'd seen several voudon ceremonies,

where drums had been used to cause the participants to enter a trance state. Once in the trance, the participant became possessed by a spirit. Shango believed that if he could induce this state in the old man, that he would be able to loosen the old man's djemon from his soul *and transfer part of it into Shango's*. His theory being that when old man died, the rest of the *djemon* would transfer into his own soul. It was more difficult to accomplish than he'd planned, but by adding some hallucinogenic ingredients to the recipe for blue absinthe, it worked. He was able to command Louis just as if he were the *djemon's* original master.

"But Shango's efforts and experiments, coupled by the increased toxicity of the absinthe formula and the old man's declining health, weakened the carny to the point where he died."

"Or was murdered," Henri said.

"That was my guess," Rhys nodded. "Louis did not transform to his *djenie* form; instead, Shango became his master. And as a side benefit, Shango discovered that the old man's spirit energy and psychic abilities had also passed to him. Shango claimed that although Louis did not change form, he gained in size; in both girth and length.

"He claimed that the transformation benefitted both of them. For his part, Louis would continue to serve Shango until his death, growing in size and stature, as Shango had promised the djemon that he would educate and make use of the creature as much as possible, thus allowing Louis to grow in size and stature to the point where he would survive his new master's death and be able to transition to human form. For eternal creatures such as *djemons*, another forty or fifty years of servitude is nothing.

"In addition, Shango discovered that by absorbing the old man's dying spirit, he had actually slowed his own aging process. He claimed to be in his mid-nineties, but looked to be closer to a man in his middle age."

I nodded uncertainly. Certainly, the man I'd met didn't look anywhere near that old, but his multicolored life lines suddenly took on a sinister meaning.

"Shango claimed that he and Louis began to seek out other demon masters. He told us he had persuaded several of them to agree to this transfer, as a sort of last will and testament process, but we didn't believe him. We had no doubt that Shango befriended them, drugged them, and taken over their *djemons* by force; just as he had done with Louis. When he offered the same service to Madame Coumlie, she declined. When he offered to pay her for the privilege, she asked him to leave.

"He told her where he was staying, and let us know that he would be in town for a few weeks, in case she changed her mind. He said that in the wake of Hurricane Katrina, much of the paranormal population had left New Orleans. He had come to Shore Haven with the intention to recruit new members for his Orissa krewe, and offer his services to other anomalous individuals who might be interested in transferring their *djemons* after death for a little extra cash."

"Madam Coumlie and I told him to pack up and get out of town. I don't think he'd ever seen anyone like Madame Coumlie's or her power over otherworldlies. I think she scared him. He left town, and until today, we never gave him another thought."

"Otherworldlies?" I asked.

"The supernatural."

"You mean anomalous individuals; like you guys."

Rhys shook his head. "No Mattie. AIs are humans with preternatural abilities. Henri and I are Otherworlders. We are able to materialize and live in this world, but we're not biological. Madame Coumlie's power was greatest over the dead and otherworldlies." His eyes met mine. "Just like you."

"What about me?"

"You radiate power like a furnace; and you haven't come into your full powers yet. You're a throwback to the age of legends; believe me, I know—I was there. Physically, you're human, but you have a soul and access to the powers of the ancients. The rules don't apply to you. You're a total wild card."

I was starting to get it; whatever *it* was. I would never be normal again. "What about the woman with him? How can Shango animate the dead?"

"He wouldn't say. But if he can insert his spirit

into the living, he may have found a way to do the same thing with the dead. There have been many cultures and religions that worshipped spirits which were able to possess bodies of the dead. Legends say that zombies still exist in Haiti and parts of the Caribbean. It's not really my area of expertise."

"How did you know she was dead?"

"No body heat," answered Henri.

"Grey fingernails," added Rhys. "She was probably wearing contact lenses, too."

"So you really think it was a zombie?" The very idea gave me the willies.

"I don't know what it was, Mattie, but it wasn't good."

"Madame said that she felt the poor thing's misery. She called Shango an abomination. Pretty tall words, for her."

"And you think there's a connection between Shango and Savanne?"

"The Savanne I knew loved her husband; they were planning on starting a family. I don't believe she would have left willingly. And she was no pushover; she was big enough to put up a good fight. I can't imagine her doing anything willingly for a character like Shango." Rhys shook his head. "No; she would not be working for him. No way."

None of us spoke, but we were all thinking the same thing. Savanne was either one of Shango's walking dead, or he'd somehow manipulated her into working for him.

Rhys spoke. "Tell us again about what you saw the other night. How did Savanne look to you? How did she act?"

"Maybe a little loud, but nothing out of the ordinary. She wanted Mimsy and I to join you two at your table, but there was something about her that bothered me. There was something wrong with her face. Did Savanne have a lot of plastic surgery?" I looked at Rhys. "I was so mad when I saw you with her, I wasn't really paying attention. I thought you were drunk. She smelled bad. I didn't want to get near her."

Both men swore.

"What?"

"Madame said that the woman who accompanied Papa Shango smelled like *djemon* and rotting corpse."

The memory of her scent returned and I gagged. "That's it! I nearly puked right there! She did, She smelled like djemon, absinthe, and rotting meat. But how? Are you saying she's a *djemon* now?" I was confused.

"I don't know," Rhys said.

I took a deep breath. "I've heard enough. We've got to do something."

"We need a plan," Rhys said. "Let me go back to the office and check my files. Maybe there's something in there that can help us."

CHAPTER 23

OKAY, SO MAYBE Shango wasn't who I thought he was, but I wasn't convinced that he was controlling Savanne. She was the dangerous one. If Luhng was right and Mimsy was dead, it had to be Savanne who'd done it.

But I didn't want to believe Mimsy was dead.

I left Rhys and Henri to argue about what to do next and headed down to the basement. The pterodactyl had made a nest for herself in the towel, and lay curled in a tight ball, sound asleep.

She stirred when I touched her, and I was glad to feel the warmth of her dark skin as I lifted her from the towel. The holes in her leathery wings, which had been shredded and tattered, were smaller, but her eyes and one side of her head was badly swollen. Still badly wounded, but at least she wasn't cold anymore. I thought that was a good sign.

I heard Henri's footsteps on the basement stairs behind me.

"Tell me, little one. Are you Annie?"

One eye opened a crack, but the pupil was

completely dilated; not even the golden iris showed.

"It's trying to transition, but it's dying," Henri said. "It's neither *djemon* nor *djenie*."

"*No!*" I curled my hands around her frail bony body. "Don't say that. As long as she's alive, Mimsy is also." I *had* to believe that. "Come on, sweetie. Yes or no. Are you Annie?"

The creature closed her eyes. *Good enough for me.*

"See? It *has* to be her. We've got to tell the police about this."

"No, Mattie, we can't. No one can know we *djenies* exist. You must know that the only way we can survive is by being invisible. The police are not the answer."

"What if they've got Lance? And Mimsy?" But from his somber expression, I knew Henri was right. Annie would not be enough to persuade anyone that Savanne and the Sinaloa Foundation had kidnapped anyone. I was pretty sure Mimsy and Lance were being held at Club Lapis, but Annie could tell me for certain. If she healed enough to talk to me, I could phone in an anonymous tip. Combined with a missing persons report, it might be enough to get a warrant for probable cause.

I called Lou Scali. He told me there had been no progress in either Lance or Mimsy's missing persons reports, and nothing that tied them to the Sinaloa Foundation.

"Stay away from that house, Mattie," Lou warned

me. "She's filed a restraining order against you. You can expect to served any day now."

"But--."

"You'll be arrested if you set foot on that property or come within fifty feet of her. You can't touch her. Just let it go."

But of course, I couldn't do that.

I walked down to the gas station on the corner of Empress and Third to call the FBI from the pay phone. The digital recording said that Agent Ted Roper was unavailable, so I left a message, giving the address of Club Lapis and saying that several large, black, winged creatures had been seen in the yard. "They look like demons," I said, and hung up without giving my name. That should be enough to send Agent Roper and his wonder-dog, Jager over there. And I was confident Jager would be able to sniff out the demon or whatever Savanne really was in no time.

As I walked back to Henri's, I started thinking. I had no way of knowing when or even if Agent Roper would bother going over to the house on Bayshore Drive, based on one anonymous tip. What if he was out of town? Or worse, what if he thought it was a crank call? Lance could be in real trouble right this very minute. The thought gnawed at me. I couldn't wait for someone else to do something. If no one else would help me rescue Lance and Mimsy, I'd have to do it myself.

By the time I got back to the house, I'd worked

myself up into a state. I brought the towel-wrapped pterodactyl up from the basement and set her on my great-grandmother's reading table, where she met with her clients.

Henri slid into the seat across from me. "What are you going to do?" He looked worried.

"I'm going to make her tell me where they are." She seemed to respond to my hands on her bare skin.

"She's too weak to talk."

I stared into Henri's eyes with steely determination. "You and Rhys keep telling me I have power over the undead. I think it's about time I started using it."

A bird fluttered against the front window and we both jumped.

It perched on the sill, stared at me and meowed. Another catbird. Dang, they were everywhere.

I gently pulled the towel away from Annie's face. She lay still. Her eyes had sunk deep into their sockets. *Oh no.* Tears filled my eyes. I leaned in and kissed her gently. "Don't you dare die on me, little one."

The catbird pecked at the window and mewled again.

"Hey, that's Jinxey," Henri said. "Your brother's *djemon.*"

Sure enough, the bird had golden eyes and no lifeline.

My heart thudded in my chest. How had I missed it? I flashed back on all the catbirds I'd heard over the past several days. *Holy crap!* He must've sent his *djemon* to find me!

CHAPTER 24

WHEN HENRI AND I went outside, the bird flew off in the direction of Bayshore Drive. With Henri holding Annie on the bike behind me, we followed him.

Jinxey the catbird; it fit. The name of our cat when we were kids. Every time I stopped at a stop sign, the bird circled back and swooped at my head. We followed it to Club Lapis, where it settled on the third-floor windowsill.

I cruised by slowly, my eyes glued to the windows on the top floor. The shades on every window were drawn down tight; it looked like no one was home, but I knew differently. And now, Jinxey confirmed it. I knew without a doubt that Lance was inside. I had to do something. I had to get him out of there.

I parked the bike on the street out front, and told Henri to wait. I jogged up the eight steps to the wide porch, but the door opened before I got a chance to ring the doorbell. It was the no-neck baldy bouncer. He handed me a folded piece of paper.

"What's this?"

"Consider yourself served, Miss Blackman. That is a restraining order prohibiting you from contact with the Sinaloa Foundation or anyone in their employ. Thanks for making it so easy. Now get off this property. The police have already been called."

He didn't have a lifeline. His eyes looked unfocused; like he wasn't really all there.

If Rhys and Henri were right, that meant he *had* to obey me.

"*Bring me Lance McNair and Miriam Wu!*" I used my voice to really put some punch into the order.

His vision seemed to sharpen, as if he noticed me for the first time. Then he slammed the door in my face.

So much for that. I should've known it wouldn't work. Or maybe Baldy had some other kind of magic working on him. I heard a siren coming closer and decided to get out while the getting was good. Better to come back tonight after Club Lapis opened. It would be dark then, and they'd be too busy to notice little old me. Sooner or later, Savanne and her friends would let down their guard, and when they did, I'd figure out what to do.

In the meantime, I had an errand to run.

Henri and I rode out to the amusement park. I had an idea that I wanted to try. Something that Rhys had said about the security guard, Charlie Crimmer, after I'd banished his *djemon*.

I'd torn his soul.

As a spirit guide, he needed his soul to attract the dead to the portal. Somehow, Annie had been torn from Mimsy's soul, just like I'd torn Snot Wad. But instead of being banished, Annie had somehow survived. If my hunch was right, the cure for Charlie Crimmer's torn soul might be Annie. And Annie hadn't had her master long enough to survive the transition from *djemon* into *djenie*. I didn't know if this would work, but I had to try it.

It took us a while to find Charlie.

We followed the path through the midway. A slight breeze coming off the lake brought the scent of cotton candy and kettle corn and memories of coming here with Lance when we were kids. The bright colors and sound effects made my heart race a little, even in the daytime.

We found Charlie Crimmer slumped down at one of the picnic tables near the corn dog stand. His grey hair was greasy, his uniform wrinkled. The dark glow of his distinctive black life-line had gone dull and ashen. His eyes, when he saw me standing there, were red-ringed and swollen.

A wave of guilt washed over me. I had done this to him. It hurt to see him this way.

"What do you want, witch?"

Behind me, I heard Henri's abrupt intake of breath, but I put my hand out. "I think I know how to fix things. Is there someplace private we can go?"

The funhouse at Heavenly Shores is called the Shriek Shanty, and it's aptly named. Not from the cries of the people inside, but the sounds of music and shrill peals of laughter and screams which blare out from loudspeakers located on the roof. Admittance costs extra, so I hadn't been inside very often; my passion for the thrill rides like the Zipper and the bumper cars made the funhouse a place worth visiting only rarely. It was a two-story building made to look like a log cabin painted brilliant yellow with candy cane stripes, green and turquoise pinwheels, and a giant, pink-lipped, carnivorous mouth for an entrance. Inside, I knew there was the hall of mirrors, an undulating floor, a spiral staircase that led to the haunted hallway on the second floor, which ended at the barrel of fun and the steep slide down and out the exit.

Charlie led Henri and me around the back to the service entrance. "This is one of the oldest buildings in town. This hall runs between the inner and outer walls of the Shriek Shanty."

We reached a door. Charlie selected a key from the ring at his belt and unlocked it. He flicked on a light switch and illuminated a set of wooden stairs leading down into the basement.

"In the 1700's the white men built their trading

post on this site, directly over a spring which was sacred to my people."

We reached the bottom of the stairs, and he flipped on another light switch. The basement was a hodge-podge mess of giant papier-mâché masks, cardboard boxes, cans of paint, and decade's worth of accumulated junk. One of the masks, a four-foot-tall jester head lolled lifelessly on its side, its gaping grin and blank eyes more terrifying than anything I'd ever seen in the haunted hall upstairs.

Charlie led me to another door, and we descended a much shorter flight of stairs into a subbasement. The floor here was hard-packed dirt, and the only light came from the dim bulb at the foot of the stairs.

"I try to keep the light low, so it won't distract the souls," he said.

It was cold down here. I shivered, wishing I'd brought my jacket.

He paused at a low, roughly circular stone wall with a hand-hewn cover of thick wooden planks. The lid, deeply inscribed with what looked like runic or aboriginal designs, looked newly painted. Dark green, but in this light I couldn't be certain.

"When I open this, you'll know what I'm talkin' about. Madame Coumlie was the one first brought me down here. "'*It's a portal,*' she told me. '*Some say to heaven, some say to hell, some say to the next incarnation. And it's not the only one. Some say there are eleven others, some say twenty-three. Some call this the river to the underworld. Doesn't matter. All that matters is that those souls who come here are given safe passage.'"*

When he lifted the lid, I could see a hard-packed dirt trail leading down into darkness. From below, wisps of what I instinctively recognized as souls began to flow up and out of the depths. They ignored Henri and Annie, and veered away from Charlie; seemingly to hover around me. The air grew thick with them, and I waved them back, away from my face, but they kept coming.

"They need someone to show them the way," Charlie said. "There's thousands of 'em down there, afraid to move on. They won't come near me no more," he added, bitterly.

I could feel their fear of him, and when I edged closer to Charlie, the hovering spirits hung back. I reached for the towel Henri was holding, and held it out to Charlie. "Here, this is for you."

He gave me a wary look. "What is it?"

I pulled the towel away from Annie's body. "This is Annie. She needs your help."

He wiped his hands on his uniform jacked and lifted her out of the towel, being careful to support her head, and tucked her into the crook of his arm. The little pterodactyl didn't respond, but it looked to me as if she leaned into his warmth.

Something changed in his posture; the pinched

expression on his face smoothed out. "What'm I supposed to do with her?"

"Unbutton your shirt. Keep her next to your skin for the next few days." I paused. If she died anyway, I'd have to find another way to heal Charlie's soul, but right now, I didn't want to think about that. If she lived, and if my hunch was right, they'd heal each other. "Sing to her. Sing her the old songs of your people."

Leaving Henri and Charlie behind, I climbed down into the portal. Charlie had given me a flashlight, and the hard-packed dirt trail, although narrow, lead around the walls and down; down to the black water below.

I don't know how long it took me to reach the bottom, but Charlie's singing chant to Annie followed me all the way down. With each step, the ghostly spirits hovered thickly around me. I could barely see my own feet.

When I reached the bottom, black water lapped with little wavelets around my ankles. I flashed the light around, impressed by the size of the cavern. This place was below the lake level, but the water had a different quality than the marine-like waters of the lake. The water here held a slight, not-unpleasant mineral tang, and was probably a good ten or twenty degrees warmer than the surface water on Lake Ontario, even in the peak of summer.

A voice echoed through the cavern, chilling me to my core. *Welcome home, mistress.*

The voice seemed to come from *beneath* the water. I cleared my throat. "Don't get your hopes up; I'm not staying." I turned to address the hovering souls, pressing up against me. I could feel both their yearning and great fear about passing beyond the portal. Something opened inside me; like a door to another place. A place of healing and joy.

This portal wasn't me, exactly. It was a portal to the legacy I had inherited from the very first woman of my line, and it led to Morta. And contrary to everything I'd ever thought or felt of death. I understood that the body belonged on the physical plane; a realm of sensation. But the realm of the dead was not of darkness and despair; it was a timeless space of spirit and peace and joy.

I'd spent my whole life thinking of death as a bad *thing*. But what I felt here was like seeing an entirely new color or flavor; a new dimension. And the portal within *me* and the one beneath the water led to the same place. As the Hand of Fate, and the living incarnation of Morta, the Goddess of Death, this was my realm. I didn't know exactly what I was supposed to say, but let the words come as they would.

"Go. Go to your rest. You are safe now. There is

nothing to fear, there is only peace."

I beckoned to the spirits, and to my astonishment, they drifted forward. They passed over and around and through me until they hovered over the water and their vapors dissipated. Each eclipsed in a spark of shining joy before fading away into the nothingness. Within minutes, they were gone.

A feeling of satisfaction and peace filled me. There was no evil in departure from the physical plane. Moreover, the goddess of death was not evil; Morta served the physical plane in a unique way, as a bridge to the next dimension. Although I had no more power over the living than any other human, my dominion ruled the non-living. This new understanding was like a drink of cool water on a hot day. I felt as if a huge weight had been lifted from my spirit.

I breathed a sigh of relief and headed back up the trail to where Charlie and Henri were waiting for me.

CHAPTER 25

THE NEXT MORNING, Mike Olsen, my supervisor, caught me as I was clocking in for work.

"Morning Mattie, you got a minute?" He had a funny expression on his face.

I slipped my timecard back into its slot. Sure what's up?" I followed him toward his office. Mike isn't just my boss; we've been friends for ages. Bowling team, babysitting for his kids, and all the rest. We'd gone through a rough patch a while back when his department budget had been pinched and I'd had a few fender-benders on the job, but since saving that guy from a heart attack, we'd been back to buddies again.

But when Mike opened the door to his office, Sheriff Reynolds was waiting, his dark eyes looking even sadder than usual.

"I'm sorry, Mattie." He slipped the handcuffs around my wrists before I even realized what was happening.

"You're under arrest for the murder of Miriam Mingmei Wu. You have the right to remain silent..."

I don't think I heard the rest. My thoughts wavered between *how could this happen* and *I can't believe she's really dead* and *thank god it's not Lance*.

Reynolds shook me gently. I realized he'd been asking the same question over and over again. "Do you understand each of these rights I have explained them to you?"

I nodded. I don't think I could have said a word, even if I wanted to.

"Having these rights in mind, do you wish to talk to us now?"

I closed my eyes and shook my head. "My lawyer's name is Fontaigne," I croaked. "I'll talk to him."

No one said anything as Reynolds led me down the aisle between the desks toward the elevator.

I'd never been in handcuffs before. I'd never been arrested before.

Sheriff Reynolds and I rode down to the first floor in silence. He gave a whispered *shit* as the elevator doors opened and the press surrounded us. I kept my head down, trying to avoid the cameras, but they were everywhere. I hated myself for crying, but couldn't seem to stop.

Reynolds finally got a couple Picston security officers to contain the crush long enough for us to make it out the back door to the parking lot.

Reynolds opened the rear door of his patrol car.

"Where are we going?"

"The county has jurisdiction. You'll be booked into the county lockup in Rochester." He put one hand on my head and the other on my back and sort of pushed me into the seat; making sure I didn't bang my head. Thick wire mesh separated the back seat from the front.

This couldn't be happening. "What makes you think I had anything to do with this? I was trying to help her!"

"They found her blood inside your burned-out apartment last night."

"There was no blood there! Talk to the FBI; agents Porter and Roper went through the whole place with a dog a couple days ago."

"That's not an alibi, Mattie. The place looked like a slaughterhouse." He slammed the door and got into the front seat.

I couldn't believe it. *How--?*

A dark green BMW pulled up beside the car and paused for a moment, the quiet engine purring. I glanced at the driver and did a double take. It was Papa Shango. He gave me a solemn nod before moving past and exiting the lot.

A chill ran up my spine. This wasn't Savanne's doing, after all. Shango had to be responsible for all of this. The murder, Lance, everything. *Lance.*

Reynolds eyed me from the rear-view mirror. "Friend of yours?"

I felt as if I were suffocating. "I didn't do it," I

protested, but my voice sounded weak. I felt weak, too. Worse, I felt *guilty*.

CHAPTER 26

THEY CUFFED ME to a table in a tiny holding cell in the basement of the Monroe County Jail. There were no windows here; nothing that would tell me whether it was night or day. Across from me, Gerard Fontaigne and his partner, a criminal defense attorney by the name of Benny Soprafino.

In contrast to Fontaigne's dapper silver fox, Benny looked like he knew his way around a tow truck. In spite of the expensive-looking suit and man-icure, his pudgy sausage fingers bore the scars and thick knuckles of a man who'd lived the seamier side of life.

Benny had brought the newspaper with him and it lay on the table between us. There was a picture of me and Sheriff Reynolds coming off the elevator at City Hall. I was cuffed and wearing my uniform; the shocked expression on face matched the headline perfectly:

PICSTON METER MAID ARRESTED
FOR MURDER

Investigation of Missing Person Leads to City Employee

I scanned the article, my face burning. They had my whole family history in there to accuse me. From my mother's extensive arrest record for drugs and prostitution, her eventual suicide in the country mental ward, to Lance's scandalous, if false, arrest as the Night Shark serial killer.

Lance. I didn't know if he was alive or dead. I didn't dare call Blix or Jinxey to find out, either. If anyone saw them, I'd never see the outside of a cell again. "I didn't do it."

"You haven't heard a word I've said." Fontaigne leaned back in his chair. "They found Miss Wu's blood splatter everywhere in your apartment. The floors; the furniture. All over the walls."

"It wasn't me. I went back once to get my clothes, and then again with the FBI. Agents Porter and Roper can confirm my story. Whoever did it came in after we left."

I thought of Shango and the knowing expression on his face as he drove past in the parking lot the day I'd been arrested. Somehow, he was responsible--but how? There was no way to tie him to any of it. And no way to get to him as long as I was in jail.

I was going to go off my rocker if I had to stay in here much longer. "You've *got* to get me out of here."

Benny folded up the newspaper and slipped it back into his briefcase. "We're working on it."

"Henri has agreed to put up the house your great-grandmother left to him as collateral," Fontaigne said. "The hearing is tomorrow. If we do get bail, it'll be expensive."

"They don't usually set bail in murder cases, but this one is circumstantial and there's no body." Benny looked at me over his half-glasses. "Any chance of one showing up?"

I stared at him. "I didn't do it. You've got to believe me. Clarence Shango is at the bottom of this mess. He's the one who killed Mimsy." *But why?* "He's got Lance locked up in that house over on Bayshore. We've got to get him out of there!"

There was a soft knock on the door and the guard stepped in. "Time's up."

I grabbed Fontagne by the wrist. "Talk to Rhys. Tell him I need to see him."

He gave me a look of surprise. "Oh. I guess you didn't know."

My heart flubbed in my chest. "Know what?"

"He's gone. Back to Scotland." Fontaigne reached into his jacket pocked at pulled out a postcard with a picture of a cartoon Scotty dog in a green and black kilt, playing the bagpipes. "I found this in my mailbox this morning."

I read the brief message, my eyes misting.

Thanks for all your help-- R

There was no postmark.

CHAPTER 27

FONTAIGNE CALLED ME from the courthouse to tell me bail had been set at two million dollars. The bad news was that Madame Coumlie's historic old Queen Anne had been appraised at less than half that amount.

I was stuck here, maybe for months, until the trial. Benny assured me that the evidence against me was circumstantial, but the trial was months away. Lance and Rhys would probably end up just like Mimsy; dead or worse.

Two days later, Benny came to see me.

Granite-faced, he pulled a business card out of his pocket and laid it on the table between us. "You know this guy?"

The name on the card was Dr. Clarence Williams. The name looked familiar.

"He told me you know him as Shango."

I slammed my hand down on the table. "He's the one that put me here! He's the one responsible for Mimsy. He's the one..." Words failed me.

Benny held his hand out in a calming gesture. "Sorry about springing this on you, but I wanted to see how you'd react. After he talked to me, I had a detective friend of mine check him out. A rather interesting fellow, and not a good way."

"What the hell does he want from me?"

"Says he wants to make a deal."

Visitor appointments to the Monroe County Jail were scheduled seven days out, so I had to wait a week before I could talk to Shango. Benny didn't want me to meet with him--or at least not yet. He had a private detective trying to figure out Shango's angle, but I didn't care.

The waiting nearly killed me. I couldn't sleep; couldn't even sit still. My mind raced as I tried to imagine what kind of deal he wanted to talk to me about. He held all the cards. I kept telling myself that as long as he wanted to talk to me, Lance and Rhys were still alive. He wanted something from me, but what? Exclusive rights to banishing *djemons*? Fine. Whatever. I didn't want the job anyway. Whatever it was, if it would get Lance and Rhys back, I'd do it.

By the time the guard came to escort me to the visitor's room, I was a bundle of nerves.

I was led to a long row of chairs seated against a

low counter, facing a thick glass partition. Visitors and prisoners spoke to each other by telephone through the inch-thick glass. The guard led me to a seat all the way at the end and handcuffed me to the table. There were dividers which gave the illusion of privacy, but Benny warned me the conversations would be recorded.

"As your lawyer, I must advise against this. He may try to trick you into saying something incriminating. Even something innocent which could be used against you. And let me tell you, this guy is pretty slick. The New Orleans Police Department has a real thick file on Clarence Williams AKA Clarence Shango and about twenty other aliases, but they've never been able to make anything stick."

"What kind of file?"

"Kidnapping, extortion, and arson, to name a few of the most recent investigations. Further back, he's been suspected of everything from grave-robbing to murder. Not a single conviction."

The thing is, he didn't *look* like bad guy. To be honest, he looked a little like a rotund Tibetan monk. And as I took as seat and picked up the phone, I still couldn't figure out those multicolored lifelines in his aura meant.

"What do you want?"

He chose his words carefully, but the gist of it was clear enough: if I would agree to his conditions, my Chinese friend would come forward and make a statement to the press. "The district attorney will be forced to drop the charges against you."

"What do you want?"

He shrugged. "I want you to leave Shore Haven. Immediately and permanently. As I told you before, I've decided to settle here and quite frankly, there isn't room for the both of us." He leaned forward in his chair, nearly touching the glass. "I want you out of town within six hours of your release. If you ever come within 250 miles of Shore Haven I will know about it."

His expression changed, and I saw the same self-satisfied smirk he used in the parking lot. The threat was clear enough.

I'd never considered living anyplace else. I'd been born in Shore Haven--I'd thought I'd live there forever. My family and friends were here. My job—well, I was probably going to have to kiss my job goodbye, after this.

"What about Lance and Rhys? You have to release them. And Mimsy too." If packing up and leaving was the price to pay for getting them back, I'd do it in a heartbeat.

A sly smile slid across his face. It didn't reach his eyes. "I don't know what you're talking about. I caution you about making false accusations against me or members of my family."

At the mention of family, a chill washed through me. Suddenly, Shango's multiple lifelines made perfect sense. "What have you done to them?"

But somehow, I already knew what he was going to say.

"I don't banish *djemons*, I take them over. The process I invented is part alchemy, part herbal, and part voudon. The process, *is not illegal*. It transfers not only the *djemon, but its master's soul as well*."

I began to tremble. "That's murder. You can't--."

"You're wrong. People can live for quite some time without their souls. Of course, they stop caring, and they do tend to go into decline rather rapidly, but that's to be expected. At some point, they just lose their will to keep living." He shook his head sadly. "At that point, only my will can keep them alive."

"You sonofabitch--."

"Whether you like it or not, Mattie, I'm the new Hand of Fate. Shore Haven and all its souls belong to me. This is a one-time-only offer to leave and never come back. Or, you can stay and be tried for murder."

CHAPTER 28

OF COURSE I agreed.

Two days later Mimsy called a press conference on the front steps of Rochester City Hall to prove she was truly alive. She claimed not to know how her blood had gotten into my apartment, but pointed out that she'd made a recent blood donation to the Red Cross and perhaps someone had taken it. She also stated that she had cut off all contact with her family over their plans for an arranged marriage for her. She then begged the press to respect her privacy and left.

A spokesman for the Red Cross immediately refuted the claim, saying they had no record of Miriam Wu making any blood donation. Ever. The district attorney had no choice but to release me.

Benny offered to pick me up when they released me from jail, but I belonged to Shango now. The limo was waiting for me outside the Monroe County Jail. The bald guy I'd seen earlier held open the door for me. I didn't see Mimsy until I got into the back seat.

I suppose I shouldn't have been surprised to see her, but I was. I'd had a lot of time to think while I was in jail. I couldn't understand why she'd colluded with Shango after I'd tried to help her. I'd never done anything to hurt her.

In the television footage, and the one grainy photo in the newspaper, she'd been dressed impeccably in a smart business suit and dark glasses. Clearly not dead at all.

But her appearance in the limo changed my anger to pity. Without sunglasses, her eyes were as opaque as those of a dead lake fish. She was wearing a lot of make-up; false eyelashes, heavy liner around the eyes, and glossy red lipstick, but it wasn't her usual look. It reminded me of one of those department-store makeovers. It didn't go with her outfit: a pair of baggy red shorts and a tight tank top. Even in the dim interior of the limo, I could see her skin was colorless and beginning to flake. She stared out the window, ignoring me. Beneath the heavy scent of perfume, she reeked of absinthe and rotting flesh.

Luhng had been right. This wasn't Mimsy anymore. Mimsy was dead.

When she finally turned to look at me, her usually sharp expression had been replaced by a dull look of total apathy. Clearly, Shango had already taken her soul. The thought filled me with dread. *Oh god, what about Lance? And Rhys...?* Rhys wasn't even human.

What did Shango want with him?

"Where's Annie?"

"What?"

I stared at her, stunned by the question. If Shango had taken her soul, and Annie had been attached to it, then theoretically, Shango controlled Annie. Yet somehow, the little *djemon* had broken free of Annie's soul; probably during the transfer of Mimsy's soul to Shango. I wanted to tell her that Annie was safe, but I had the feeling the question hadn't come from Mimsy. More like Shango wanted to know how Mimsy's *djemon* had gotten away from him.

"I have no idea. Have you tried calling her?"

A ghastly grimace stretched across Mimsy's face. She spoke slowly, as if she had trouble pronouncing the words. She rubbed her chest, the half-moon beds of her fingernails were blue-black. "It makes Papa mad when she won't come."

She leaned toward me, her eyes like a blind man's, her voice thick with yearning. "He won't let me go until Annie comes back." She grabbed my wrist; the touch of her cold hands and grey fingernails convinced me that this dead thing wasn't Mimsy anymore. A zombie, maybe, but not alive.

And never would be again.

I hoped Annie was safely attached to Charlie Crimmer by now. I thought about Jinxey and what that meant for Lance. Jinxey was still attached to Lance;

still under Lance's control. Was he like Mimsy or had he managed to fight the process? And what about Rhys? *What was Shango up to?*

I wrapped my arms around myself, chilled with the realization of what I'd really agreed to.

CHAPTER 29

THEY TOOK ME to the Greyhound bus station in downtown Rochester, and the bald-headed driver, who told me his name was Evan, handed me a one-way bus ticket to San Francisco. Mimsy stayed in the car as Evan escorted me to the bus and watched to make sure that when it departed, I was on it.

All I had with me was my driver's license and ten bucks. Even if I'd managed to borrow a phone, Henri didn't have a car, and couldn't drive, anyway. There was no point in trying to call anyone from work, either. I remembered the looks on their faces when I'd been arrested. I'd never go back.

I sat back into the seat, numbed by the thought that Shango had won. He held all the cards now, there was nothing I could do about Lance or Rhys. Or Mimsy. He'd taken everything from me. My home, my friends, even my only family. And he'd done it so easily.

Whether you like it or not, Mattie, I'm the new Hand of Fate now.

He didn't understand. And I'd been so self-absorbed, I'd practically invited him in to take over.

Shore Haven and all its souls belong to me.

What an arrogant prick. If I was really the living incarnation of Morta, I needed to start owning it. He had no idea what he was up against.

By the time we pulled into Cleveland, my mind was made up. I made my way to the pay phones, planning to call Benny, but a poster for New Orleans Mardi Gras caught my eye. An inset map showed the French Quarter, and I could see the Algiers neighborhood was just across the river. It took me a minute to remember where I'd seen that familiar name before.

It was on Shango's business card. I didn't remember the exact street address, but I remembered the name of the street. Lamarque Street, Algiers, Louisiana.

I went to the ticket window and exchanged my ticket, getting more than a hundred bucks back as a refund. The bus for New Orleans left in twenty minutes. I went to the pay phone and made a call to Benny. I told him what I needed and told him I'd call him back when I got to New Orleans.

Shango had told me people could live for a while without their souls, but didn't say how long. If I were to have any chance of rescuing Lance and Rhys and whoever else he had locked up in that house down on Bayshore, I needed to find out what I was up against. Benny had given me Clarence Williams' exact address on Lamarque Street.

When I first met him, Shango had told me he needed to start over, but he'd been pretty vague on the reasons, and upstate New York was an awfully big change from Louisiana.

The answers were waiting for me in Algiers, Louisiana.

CHAPTER 30

IN SPITE OF their proximity on the map, the French Quarter and Shango's neighborhood in Algiers were nothing alike. Where the historic center of the French Quarter was filled with character and beautiful brick and wrought iron and bright spots of color glimpsed from secret gardens, Shango's address was nothing more than a run-down warehouse in a derelict neighborhood. No trees, no gardens, no fancy restaurants. Just humid, weed-filled lowlands, as devoid of trees and landscaping as any place I'd ever seen.

A city bus took me from the main terminal across the bridge to Algiers. The bus let me off three blocks from the river, in a nearly deserted area which seemed to be full of nothing more than big, hulking warehouses. Four short blocks later, I found the gray building at Shango's address. There was no sign out front, and no windows on the first floor. Nothing to give me any hint about was inside. I double-checked the address to be sure.

The battered yellow front door was locked and padlocked from the *outside*. Around back, an armored metal garage door guarded the loading dock. I spotted two cameras aimed at the alley. Shango's, I noticed, was the only building along the alley with security cameras.

There was a second-floor window and fire escape, but no way to reach it from the alley. I walked around the neighborhood, trying to figure out a way in and hit the jackpot.

A couple of window washers were cleaning the windows at the All Saints church, a block away. Their truck was parked in the parking lot, out of view. I thought of taking one of their ladders, but found a long pole with a hook on the end, which ended up being perfect for grabbing the lower rung of the fire escape and bringing it down. It wouldn't lower all the way to the ground, but I managed to jump up and scramble my way to the landing.

The window was painted shut. Or warped, it didn't matter. The glass shattered easily with my shoe, and after clearing away the shards, I was in.

I was already sweating; the office was hot and smelled musty. I looked around, trying to get my bearings.

If this was Shango's office, it looked like he lived here, too. There was a dusty sofa on one wall; covered with a tangle of yellowed sheets. A heavy wooden desk with the calendar turned to December of last year. I rifled through the unlocked drawers, but there was little inside which would lead me to think it belonged to Shango. I did find a big honkin' yellow-handled screwdriver in the bottom drawer, and grabbed it. Holding it in my hand made me feel better.

But there wasn't much else in the room. The two wooden file cabinets held nothing; not even a scrap of a receipt. Likewise, I found nothing in the tiny attached bathroom. But when I tried to leave, I found the door locked. Again, from the outside. Weird.

Lucky for me, I had the big honkin' screwdriver and knew how to use it. In less than five minutes, I'd pulled the pins out of the hinges, and I was out on the landing, gazing down into the open warehouse space. The light was fading, and most of the windows were covered with newspaper. I tried the light switch, but the power was off.

Walking down the iron staircase, I paused, as a shiver passed through me. The set-up wasn't so different from Club Lapis.

But here, there were two low platforms, like stages, set up with huge speakers and stereo equipment. The walls were covered with dozens of old mattresses, standing on end, giving the large space a claustrophobic feel; like something out of a padded cell at a psych ward, only much bigger. The mattresses were old, stained, and grey. Several had been shredded at some point and the stuffing pulled out, or patched with duct tape.

In the middle of the room, two sturdy wooden chairs had been bolted a heavy wooden platform. The chairs sat back-to-back, each facing the massive speakers, and each had thick woven straps at the armrests and legs. Not a good sign. I remembered the disorientation I felt when the drumming started up that night at Club Lapis. I wondered if sound or music had something to do with Papa Shango's 'method' for banishing *djemons*.

As I neared the stage at the back of the room to examine the stereo equipment, the heavy, unmistakable reek of *djemon* assaulted me.

I froze. I hadn't seen any alarms; no little green lights or electronics. Not even a smoke detector. But by the stink of *djemon*, I was finally certain I was in the right place. This warehouse *must* belong to Shango. But if he'd left his djemons in charge of security, I could be in big trouble.

"Hello? Is anybody here?"

Stupid, but it slipped out before I could stop myself. Besides, the purpose of the mattresses suddenly made sense. They deadened the sound.

Cautiously, I moved toward the stage and examined the sound equipment. The old-fashioned reel-to-reel tape player and CD-player hadn't seen use in weeks, if not months. Everything was covered in a thick layer of dust.

Behind the six-foot tall speakers, a gap in the mattresses led to another door; this one likewise padlocked from the outside. The smell of *djemon* was stronger here. I had no doubt this would lead to the basement, and the answers I needed.

The lock was attached to a simple hasp, and I used my trusty screwdriver to unscrew the hasp. The doorknob turned easily, and as I opened the door I was struck by a chilly force of basement air, redolent with the smell of *djemons*. There was more than one down there.

I hesitated, but my determination to find out everything I could about Shango drove me forward. I knew the only chance I had of rescuing my friends would be found in that basement.

I tried the light switch at the top of the stairs, and this time, it worked.

CHAPTER 31

THE BASEMENT WAS smaller than I expected, with a low ceiling, barely six feet high. The air was damp and fetid. Six closed, but not locked metal crates lined the wall opposite the stairs. He must have caged these *djemons* before he left. At his command, they'd stay down here until he died.

One cage stood empty, but the others housed a collection of good-sized *djemons*. Each one big enough to survive the transition to *djeni* at the death of their master. There was a three-eyed toad form; so grossly fat, it was unable to turn around in the cage. A vile-looking serpent, a lizard, a rat-like rodent as big as a washing machine, and a sphinx. The sphinx looked only slightly smaller than my great-grandmother's *djemon*, Oneiri. They stared at me with something like recognition in those watchful, yellow eyes.

Shango had managed to pull their souls from their masters into himself. It was the only thing that could account for his multiple lifelines. Their original masters were dead, most likely. But if he controlled them, why were they caged here in this basement? Why had he left them behind? I needed to find out.

Maybe these guys wouldn't talk to me. But I had to try. I decided to start with the sphinx.

"What is your name?"

It made a face, as if offended, but didn't answer. Perhaps Shango had forbidden them to speak. Or maybe, and I thought this was far more likely, it only answered to its master.

"Answer me. I am the Hand of Fate."

"I know who you are."

The voice was neither obviously male nor female; the growled tone sent a thrilled shiver through me. Haughty and cold, this creature was as big and powerful-looking as a lion. I had no doubt it *could* tear me to pieces, but for some reason, I didn't think it would.

"Who is your master?"

"I obey Shango."

"But he not the one who named you."

The answer came as a hiss. "*No.*"

"Tell me how this happened."

The toad shuffled closer to the bars. After swallowing several gulps of air, he belched. "*Drum! Drum!*"

"The equipment upstairs?"

The lizard clawed frantically at the heavy grate across the front of his cage. "*He sssteals sssoulsss.*"

They were all getting agitated. The sphinx had her ears laid back. I knew she would tell me, even as I could see she didn't want to. I motioned for the others to be still.

I took a deep breath and reached for the portal in my head; the one to Morta. "Tell me your story, Sorroh." The fact that I knew her name didn't seem to surprise her.

She curled her lion-like tail around her massive paws like some overgrown housecat.

"My mistress named me on the event of her third birthday. All the women of her village claim their djinn in this way. We grew together in strength and wisdom. In the islands it is easier to be discreet. But when she came to this country to attend to her advanced studies, she wisely kept me hidden on other planes. There I could observe and share her learning without being seen. After her schooling, she taught at the University, and we interacted less and less. She fell in love and married, as humans do. Her new husband was a pilot."

"Your mistress is Savanne, isn't it?"

Sorroh nodded. *"Shango sat next to her on a flight home from a visit her family in Jamaica. He was quite taken with her, and pursued her relentlessly, even as she told him she was married and flat refused him. He followed her and even had their apartment bugged; which was how he found out about me.*

"The serpent is the oldest of us." Sorroh nodded

her head toward the large snake *djemon* at the other end of the row of cages. "*He is mad, but possesses the power of speech. The others, due to the shapes of their mouths have a difficult time conversing. When Shango saw how easily my mistress and I conversed, he had to have me. He waited until her husband was out of town, and then kidnapped her; keeping her drugged until he brought her here.*

"*Shango is a practitioner of the voudon. It is a form of magic familiar to my mistress and her people, but he has twisted it and reworked it to suit his purposes. He has perfected a powerful, but slow-acting hallucinogenic poison that gradually destroys the ability of the spirit to maintain its hold in the body. Combined with trance-inducing rhythms of drumming, the soul is loosened, and he uses a strange hook-like instrument to lift the soul from the body of his subject. Once the drumming stops, the detached soul is attracted by Shango's more powerful, multithreaded aura and becomes anchored there.*

"*In the beginning, she fought him. My mistress is strong and powerful, but the poison in the absinthe numbed her mind and eventually she became addicted to it, needing more and more every day. Over time, she lost all her will to fight him, and within a few weeks it was done.*

"What does Shango want them for?"

"*He believes that by taking over the souls*

210

of others, he can become immortal. Through his experimentation, he has discovered that only the souls of djemon masters can survive his transfer process. Without their souls, our masters do not live very long; although he has recently found a way to animate their corpses until decay eventually takes over. Once he has their souls, he controls us as well."

"So why did he leave you here? What does he want in Shore Haven?"

Sorroh favored me with a haughty expression.

"He wants what all djemon masters want. He uses the others to steal for him, but from me, he seeks knowledge of the underworld. Your world, Morta. He wants to know the dark secrets of the universe, especially those which he can use to his own advantage"

She told me Shango had to move because the whole block was going to be torn down to make way for condominiums.

"Many djemon masters lived in the parts of the city which were hardest hit by the hurricane, Katrina, and they fled the area. Shore Haven has a good population of djemon masters with large djemons; their souls are perfect for his needs. And unlike the New Orleans Police Department, his name is unknown to law enforcement in Shore Haven. After he achieves his goal of immortality, he intends to make himself a god to an immortal race."

"He's crazy." I remembered the odd, stretched

look of the skin on Savanne's face, and the grey color of Mimsy's fingernails the last time I'd seen her. "What about the people whose souls he's taken? Is there any way to bring them back?"

"Dead is dead, Morta. You know that."

Oh god. My thoughts went to Lance. What would happen if Shango had already stolen his soul? I could only hope Lance was still alive. Jinxey was my only proof of that. What about the others? How many were there? Could I get them back their souls before they died? I considered Shango's multi-colored lifelines and how easily the Hand of Fate could break them. Just a snap of a finger.

"What would happen if I broke Shango's multithreaded life line? Would everyone die?"

Yes. The humans would die.

"He's taken a *djenie* friend of mind. Do you know why?"

For the first time, the haughty expression on Sorroh's face changed. She looked frightened. *"I do not know. Shango is obsessed with immortality, but djenies can be killed. Perhaps he thinks to somehow use the djenie in some way."* When she shuddered, her black feathers rustled like heavy satin. *"He has experimented on us, but we are not djenie."*

"How do I stop him?"

"Kill him and we will be free. Free to become djeni."

"His lifeline is interwoven with the souls of many

humans, including my friends and family. If I kill him, they will die as well."

From the far end of the cages, the serpent began throwing itself against the front of the cage, hissing. "*Kill him! Kill, kill, kill!*"

The thought of allowing this corrupted creature to transform into a *djeni* nauseated me. "Calm yourself, *Louis*." Instantly, the snake demon shrank away from the front of the cage. His name had come to me as easily as Sorroh's. The rat-thing was *Antoine*, the Lizard *Tarikki*; the bloated toad, *Blork*.

Another reason not to kill Shango. If he died, all these angry *djemons* would transform into uncontrollable, angry *djeni*.

The only way to save Lance and the others was if Shango released their souls willingly. Given his obsession with immortality, I didn't believe this was something he was likely to do. I would have to offer him something better than another human soul.

The answer, when it came, brought me no relief at all.

CHAPTER 32

I TOOK A cab from the Greyhound bus station to Doc's Garage. I'd called ahead and agreed to sell him my bike in exchange for the repairs to Trusty Rusty; he'd even thrown in a new black paint job. Doc had worked his mechanic's magic and my ancient Honda now hummed like a satisfied alley cat. No one would recognize me in this late-model, respectable Civic. I even got a little cash back out of the deal.

The look on Henri's face when I came through the back door of Madame Coumlie's house was priceless. He looked at me like I was a ghost. And maybe I was.

"Where have you been? Rhys is gone too."

"Yeah, I know. You still have those old costumes of Madame Coumlie's in the basement?"

"What? No, I had the best of them cleaned. They're hanging in your closet upstairs."

"Come on. We've got a show to do." I raced up the staircase ahead of him. "And I need a thorough tutoring session on *djemons*, and *djenie*."

Henri caught me by the arm at the top of the stairs. "What are you going to do?"

"Shango is obsessed with immortality. He's stealing souls so he can live their life spans. He doesn't understand that I possess the immortal soul of the Hand of Fate. I'm going to offer him Morta's soul in exchange for theirs."

His pale blue eyes stared into mine. "You can't do this." For the first time, I saw how very human he had become. There was pain there. And worry. And love. "*Your soul belongs to Morta.*"

"If there's any other way, I'd love to hear about it." I couldn't let him stop me. If I didn't go now, I might not have the nerve.

"He'll never believe you."

"Oh yes he will. He only knows me as Madame Coumlie's great grand-daughter. He doesn't know I've got more power than she ever did. I'm going to convince him that I'm the living incarnation of Morta, I'm gonna need to dress the part."

Madame Coumlie was a tiny woman; one of the little people. The costumes she wore nearly a century earlier had been well-preserved, and Henri found me a couple of pieces that fit surprisingly well over my plain black, sleeveless leotard. The worn leather jacket was short; more like a bolero on me; dyed deepest indigo with the moon phases embroidered in silver threads down the back, and what Henri called Egyptian cartouches on the notched lapels and down the sleeves. I found a purple and orange striped tulle skirt that fit as a miniskirt. I wore it over black fishnet tights and my kick-ass black leather biker boots.

I told Henri about what I'd learned from Savanne's *djemon*, Sorroh. When I described the tool Sorroh told me Shango had used to snag the souls, he uttered a sharp yell and raced down the stairs to the basement, only to return a moment later with the ankh.

The ankh with the sharpened point and hook on the long end. *A gift from the deity to the mortal incarnation of her line.*

Henri was shaking as he handed it to me. "Don't you think this looks like the tool the sphinx described? Rhys was certain its purpose is ritual."

The metal and bone instrument warmed to my hand. I hefted it; the weight was well-balanced. Good for bashing skulls, if nothing else. There was a *rightness* about the feel of it Maybe the hook was used to snag the soul.

Yes. Another portal in my head cracked open. I was supposed to have this.

A certainty came over me. Whatever I was going to do, it was the right thing. Henri wanted to come with me, but I told him he would only be another distraction. Instead, I called for Blix, and we set off in my newly-painted black Honda to meet with Papa Shango on his own turf.

CHAPTER 33

A THROBBING SENSATION coming up through the floor brought me back to consciousness. My head pounded painfully with each beat. I felt muzzy and nauseated. The air was stuffy; redolent with the stink of stale absinthe, urine and vomit.

I struggled to sit up in the near-darkness. My hands were cuffed and chained to the frame of an iron cot, bolted to the floor. I was naked beneath an oversized man's tee-shirt. Not mine.

The single small window in the room had been covered with foil, but there were a couple of places where daylight seeped through the cracks. As my eyes adjusted, I realized I was in a bedroom. Based on the slope of the roof, maybe the attic.

The cuffs were too tight to slip out of; the chain just long enough to allow me to reach the slop bucket on one side of the bed, and a plastic jug of water on the other. I fumbled for the jug and managed to twist off the top. Water spilled down my chin and shirt as I drank, but I didn't care. I couldn't remember ever being so thirsty.

Bargaining with Shango had seemed like such a good idea. He hadn't believed me at first. Not until he called Sorroh and the sphinx confirmed that I was the living legacy of the goddess Morta. After that, they grabbed me and forced that nasty absinthe down my throat.

My skin ached in every pore. I ran my hands over my body, feeling the same raised bites I'd seen on Rhys. Shango had had Louis, the snake *djemon* bite me over and over. With each bite, Louis sucked deeply, as if trying to both inflict venom and feed off me at the same time. Shango said it was part of the process.

"The absinth merely loosens your soul, Mattie. Louis's bite pulls it to the surface where I can snag it with my hook. I carved it myself from the femur bone of a soulless man, so as the victim nears death, the soul rises and is attracted to the bone implement."

I finally realized why his multicolored lifeline looked so strange to me. It wasn't just one lifeline, it was many; each thread entwined like a rope, each thread a stolen soul.

"It's a tricky technique, and although I lost a lot in the beginning, I've already extended my life by six lifetimes. I rarely make a mistake any more, although your friend Mimsy was a regrettable casualty. Imagine what I'll gain from taking yours."

I shuddered at the memory.

Three other beds shared the room with me; I could just make out the lumps of bodies in the two across the room.

"Hey! Wake up," I whispered, as loud as I dared. "Lance, is that you? Rhys!"

No one stirred. The cot closest to me was empty, with only a wadded up blanket and bucket to indicate there had been a previous occupant. I guessed the mute throbbing from below originated in the basement, where no doubt my fellow captive was undergoing Louis and Shango's special attentions.

"Blix," I whispered. "I summon you."

My little *djemon* appeared immediately. Even in the murk, his yellow eyes glowed reassuringly. Damn, it was good to see him. His little body quivered attentively, awaiting my command. I hesitated. How much could one Chihuahua-sized *djemon* do? I couldn't very well send him to the police.

Now that he had me, Shango would not, could not be stopped. The utter hopelessness of the situation weighed on me like dirt in the grave. He would take Lance's soul, and the souls of anyone he chose, simply because he could. The empty expression on Mimsy's face haunted me. What if he managed to get Morta's legacy? What would happen if Shango got his hands on that kind of power?

I pounded my thigh with my fist. I'd frittered all my chances away. There had to be something else I could do. Whatever it was, I better hurry up and think of it.

The door opened and the sudden overhead light blinded me. I hid my eyes in my shoulder, but not before I'd seen who it was. I banished Blix, but it was too late.

Savanne and Shango had already seen him.

"I told you she had a demon," Savanne gloated. "You didn't believe me." She approached the bed and sat on my legs.

I blinked rapidly, my eyes unaccustomed to the bright light. The thing sitting on me wasn't human. Something was wearing her body like a suit.

Baldy Evan dragged Rhys's unconscious body into the room. He was wearing nothing other than a pair of cut-offs. He was filthy; his hair and beard matted with blood. Baldy chained him to the empty cot beside me, I could see every inch of his exposed skin was covered with more fresh bites.

Anger surged through me as I realized that Rhys had been telling the truth. I squirmed beneath Savanne, fighting to kick her, but she weighed a lot. She wasn't alive, but wasn't dead, either.

"What do you want Rhys for?"

"I've never had a real *djenie* to play with. I'm trying to extract his soul," Shango said.

I smothered a gasp. *He didn't know djenis don't have souls. Whatever Sorroh and the others had told him, they hadn't told him everything. Or maybe he just hadn't asked the right question.*

Baldy unlocked my chains, but my hands were still cuffed. With the light on, I could see Lance and another man chained to the other cots. My heart leapt at the sight of my brother.

Lance's eyes were closed. He didn't move.

They brought me down to the basement. To Club Lapis. The place was empty; no customers, and nothing cooking in the kitchen. The dining tables and chairs had been pushed to the side against one wall. In the center of the room, surrounded by speakers almost identical to what I'd seen at the warehouse in Algiers, was a Stonehenge-like circle of six-foot tall speakers arranged in a ring around a sort of a barber's chair.

The Savanne thing and Evan strapped me in like I was no more bother than a two year-old having a tantrum. The thing that looked like Savanne wasn't like Mimsy. Mimsy without her soul had been a pitiful, weak creature. This thing--.

Savanne was still breathing, so she wasn't dead yet, but she had no lifeline, and her *djemon* Sorroh belonged to Shango now. They both did. Louis had somehow gotten *inside* her dying body.

The idea hit me in a flash. As the Hand of Fate, I could banish him. *Louis would have to obey me!*

"Louis! Louis, listen to me! I command--."

But Shango shoved the gag into my mouth before I could get the words out. I screamed and fought, but it was too late. They'd strapped me into the chair, gagged me, and Shango was already over at the controls, wearing ear protection for what I knew was coming.

The sound of drums boomed through the speakers.

My bones vibrated with the beat; my face felt numb. I tried to concentrate, but the relentless cadence pulsed and throbbed, filling my brain with mush. I felt my focus slipping; slipping *away*.

Shango smiled that beatific smile of his, and approached with hospital IV drip bag filled with the pale blue absinthe. Deftly, he inserted the hollow needle into a vein in my arm, and there wasn't one thing I could do to stop him.

CHAPTER 34

"PSST. MATTIE, WAKE up. Psst."

Rhys crouched on the floor between our two beds. Chained as we were, we couldn't reach each other. Shango had cuffed my hands behind my back so I couldn't get the gag out of my mouth, but I squirmed to the floor and scooted as close to Rhys as I could.

He looked even worse than I remembered. I didn't know how long I'd been here, but I knew he'd been here longer. Even his inhuman ability to heal hadn't helped him. He was covered with fresh puncture bites and bruises. His contact lenses were gone; his eyes glowed yellow in the dim light of morning streaming through a scratch in the foil-covered attic window.

Across the room, Lance sat hunched over the side of his cot, his hands cupped around Jinxey as if the little bird were a warm coal. He'd lost so much weight, I barely recognized him.

His life line was gone.

It had been there yesterday.

I slumped forward; my heart breaking. Tears ran down my cheeks. I was too late.

In the forth cot, the man I knew only as Chen lay on his back with his arm over his eyes. He'd travelled all the way from China at the request of Mimsy's mother and Leung to meet Mimsy, his chosen wife. From his fading aura, I could tell he was of a *djragon* family, just as Mimsy had been. They'd used Mimsy as bait to bring him to them.

Rhys's voice sounded from a long ways away. "Mattie. Pay attention."

I shook my head. Nothing mattered any more. Shango had Lance's soul. Before long, he'd be one of the shambling dead; just like Mimsy.

"Stretch out toward me as far as you can. I think I can unbuckle the strap holding the gag in your mouth."

A pounding ache echoed the drums in my head.

"Come on, honey. Let me help you."

It wasn't fair. None of this. I grunted through the gag, but Lance didn't even look up. I'd been so wrong about everything. I should have done more for Lance. I should have been there for him. I should have believed Rhys. Both men loved me and I let them down. I'd broken my oath and denied my legacy and now I couldn't help them.

I squirmed closer to Rhys, unable to lift my head from the floor, even if I wanted to. I shuddered with the memory of what Shango had done to me last night. Now that he had Lance, he seemed to be more determined than ever.

I shoved my feet against the legs of the cot, pushing myself as close to Rhys as I could, but the chains weren't long enough. Rhys scooted around and started working at the buckle with his bare toes. The gag was some sort of a rubber ball held in place with a buckle at the back of my head. My hair kept getting tangled, but he kept working at it.

With the possible exception of Rhys, none of us would last much longer. With every yank on the buckle, I felt my hopes starting to rise, only to be dashed gain. The buckle was too tight. I lowered my chin to give him better access.

My lips and jaw were in agony; I doubted I could speak even if he managed to get the gag out of my mouth. Even if I did manage to use Shango's *djemons* against him, how would I stop him? He had so many lifelines twisted into his; what would happen to the poor souls of his victims who were still alive? Victims like Lance and Chen?

Rhys gave a low grunt of frustration as his toes cramped. "Shit. I almost had it."

As I allowed my anger to grow within me, I could feel the power build up behind that door in my mind. What would happen if I opened it? What if I let Morta out? But I already knew the answer. *People would die.*

Killing Shango would only kill everyone whose

souls he'd stolen.

There had to be another way.

There was a hard jerk at the back of my neck, and the gag came loose.

I gasped and rubbed my head against the rough wood floors, and the gag was gone. I squirmed into a sitting position.

"I'm sorry I didn't believe you about Savanne." The words tumbled out, as the tears streaked down my face. "I didn't understand that you couldn't lie to me. I love you, Rhys. I didn't ask you to stay because I was afraid you'd stay because I'm the Hand of Fate, not because of me."

"Easy, Mattie. They're just downstairs. We need the keys. Jinxey doesn't have the right kind of claws to fetch the keys. We need Blix."

"Oh you're right. Blix, where are you?"

In an instant, my little *djemon* appeared in front of me.

"Blix bring the keys for the handcuffs, but whatever you do, don't get caught. Don't let them see you. And Hurry."

An instant later, he winked out of sight.

"Whatever happens, you gotta kill him. You've got to kill Shango." Lance's tortured whisper startled me.

"I can't; he's got your soul now. And the lives and souls of others tangled up in his life line. If I kill him, they'll die too. *And so will you!*"

Rhys grunted. "So what's the plan?"

"I've got an idea, but I don't know how to loosen the other souls from his lifeline. We need that Ankh, Rhys. The one Henri showed you in the basement. Henri and I figured out what it is."

"What are you talking about?"

"Shango uses the music and drugs to loosen the soul's hold on a mortal's lifeline. He has a special hook carved from human bone that he uses to snag the soul and extract it from its host. If we can stop him, I think I can use that Ankh to extract the souls of the living from Shango's lifeline. But we have to find it. It's somewhere here in the house."

"What?" Rhys stared at me. "Why did you bring it here?"

I shrugged. "It went with the outfit."

Rhys stared at me, a slow grin spreading across his ravaged face. "You always know just what to say to lighten the mood."

At that moment, Blix reappeared with the keys.

CHAPTER 35

THE OLD HOUSE creaked with every step; there was no way we could get down the stairs and out the front door quickly without making enough noise to wake the dead. We were three floors up; even if the windows weren't painted shut, it was too far to jump. We crouched on our cots, trying to decide the best strategy.

There had to be at least two people in the house; Shango and his son, Evan. But Shango commanded at least five very large djemons. Lance would be no help to us, as he was barely able to walk. Even Jinxey appeared listless. I told Lance to tuck her beneath his shirt to keep her warm and next to his skin. We didn't have much time.

Rhys and I would go first. The noise would rouse the household, while Lance and Chen hung back until the action started; then Chen would make his escape while Lance searched for the ankh.

Barefoot, we made less noise, but Louis sounded

the alarm before we reached the second floor landing. In snake form, Louis was truly a frightening apparition, His head was as big as mine. His eyes glowed yellow with an intelligent, malevolent gleam.

I didn't dare hesitate.

"Hear me and obey, Louis. I am the Hand of Fate. I hereby banish you from all physical and metaphysical earthly planes, never to return."

Nothing happened.

Louis hissed and struck at me, open-fanged. He missed.

"Shit," I said.

Rhys, pulled me back, and we retreated from the approaching *djemon*. "What happened?" He asked.

"I've got to be in contact with Shango."

"That's only to banish him. Come on, Mattie, do something. You can command his movements!"

Louis slithered forward again, backing us toward the stairs. I pushed the door inside my head open a little wider. A dark chill spread through me.

"Louis, I command you to freeze!"

Louis held perfectly still, his mouth agape; pearls of milky poison oozing from the tips of his fangs.

One of the bedroom doors opened and Shango stepped into the hallway. He'd dressed hurriedly; and wore only shorts and a mis-buttoned Hawaiian shirt. In one hand he held Morta's ankh.

"To your cage, Louis." Shango might have been

asking someone at to pass the cream.

Before I could react, Louis disappeared. I swore silently. Of course Shango could countermand any command I would give his djemon, and short of gagging him, there wasn't much I could do about it.

Rhys hurled himself towards Shango, and the two men went down. Shango outweighed Rhys, but Rhys was a far better fighter than the demon master. The ankh went flying, and I rushed to grab it. Once in my hand, Morta's power flowed through me like an angry river. I felt invincible.

Shango shouted for Sorroh, but Rhys landed a punch to Shango's diaphragm. He dropped him like a rock, all the fight gone out of him. He rolled on the carpet, gasping for breath.

The sphinx appeared, and I ordered her to stay. Evan stumbled out of his room, still half asleep, and Rhys and I both jumped on him, holding him down until Chen brought down the hand cuffs and we handcuffed the both of them.

CHAPTER 36

WITH BOTH SHANGO and Evan cuffed, we dragged Shango down to the basement and strapped him into the same chair where he'd tortured all of us. Chen and Rhys were all for dishing out a little physical payback on their torturer, but I was terrified that every moment that passed increased the chances that we wouldn't be able to rescue Lance or anyone else's souls. Lance's color looked worse every time I looked at him.

I sent Chen to go get help.

"I'm only going to say this once. Release the souls you've stolen. From my brother and Mimsy and anyone else."

His grin held no warmth at all. "It's too late for Mimsy." He nodded toward Lance, slumped on a chair in the corner. "And if you kill me, your bother will die."

"Fine. Have it your way." Rhys was already at the bar, preparing an intravenous bag of absinthe, but I already knew what to do. I needed to weaken Shango, not kill him. I shoved a cloth napkin from one of the dining tables into his mouth and summoned Sorroh.

The sphinx *djemon* appeared immediately. She looked somber, almost as if she knew what was coming.

"Hear me and obey, Sorroh. I hereby banish you from all physical and metaphysical earthly planes, never to return."

Sorroh's shriek of agony was echoed by a gut-wrenching groan from Shango, as he fought against the straps which held him. Sorroh's screams had us all putting out hands over our ears. The *djenie* convulsed, biting at her legs. A moment later, she disappeared.

I'd never banished such a large *djemon* before. Light-headed, I broke out into a sweat.

One of the threads within Shango's multicolored lifeline dimmed. *Savanne's*. It didn't go out but I had no idea if it meant she was still alive. I steeled myself to Shango's agonized moans, watching Lance for any reaction.

"Give my brother back his soul, Shango or I swear I'll banish every single one of your djemons until your soul is nothing but tatters. Let it go."

He glared at me and shook his head.

This time, I summoned Blork, the ghastly three-eyed toad. It disappeared with a gigantic belching croak.

With Blork gone, Shango's skin took on a grey pallor. Age spots covered his bald scalp and hands. He looked like a man well into his eighties. The lifelines which encircled him were not so tightly wound. I thought it might be possible to disentangle them.

I removed the gag and picked up the ankh. The warm, solid weight of the ancient metal in my hand felt reassuring.

"Last chance, you shit. Give back the souls you stole."

He shook his head. "I don't know how. I only know how to take them. You're killing me. I promise I'll never come back. Just let me go."

"Not gonna happen." Lance's soul glowed a pale neon blue. I tried to slip the hook of the ankh beneath it, but there were too many others twisted around it; I was afraid to break any of them.

The only way to free it was to banish all of Shango's *djemons*. Each banishment would damage the soul attached to it. On the other hand, each would bring Shango to a new level of pain. It should have bothered me more than it did, but I didn't care. Morta's cold rage fueled my own. When I banished Tarikki the lizard, I staggered. I had to sit down. Banishing these big guys used up a lot of juice.

Shango bucked and grunted like a pig, but after Antoine the giant rat was gone, he was too weak to fight anymore. He'd shrunk onto a tiny, wrinkled old man. His once multicolored lifeline consisted of only four thin threads now. Lance and Savanne's, souls, plus his own and the soul of Louis' original master.

Lance lay curled up in a fetal position on the floor,

his hands still clutching Jinxey. His skin looked so pale.

I didn't think Shango could stand much more. I reached for the ankh. Now that he had fewer souls entangled in his lifeline, there was more slack between them. I slipped the ankh beneath Lance's pale blue line and managed to snag it.

Rhys and I must've smelled the smoke at the same time. Our eyes met.

"Keep trying," he said. "I'll go check the kitchen."

Shango's twisted, multithreaded lifeline existed entirely within his aura, like a giant lasso. It was still twisted within the threads of the others. I knew from experience that if I pulled too hard, his lifeline would break; and if that happened he *would* die. Using the hook of the ankh to hold Lance's lifeline separate from the others, I slowly ran my hand along its length; carefully untwisting it. But there were still too many threads.

The smoke was getting thicker.

"Louis, I summon you!"

Instantly, the *djemon* snake appeared before me. His posture was meek, but his amber eyes glowed with an inner madness. I wasn't fooled.

"If you banish Louis, it'll kill me," Shango threatened, his voice weak. "I'm not strong enough. If I die, so will your brother. Let me go."

Without his soul, Lance would die anyway.

Lance coughed weakly. Upstairs, the smoke

detectors began to shriek.

I drew in a deep breath and opened the door to Morta a little wider. Immediately, her cold power filled me.

Thrilled me.

"Hear me and obey, Louis. I am the Hand of Fate. I hereby banish you from all physical and metaphysical earthly planes, never to return."

Shango screamed as if his heart were being torn from his chest. I watched the copper lifeline of Louis's former master break apart and disappear, and Shango's own lifeline began to dim. I didn't have much time.

Ignoring Shango's cries, I took hold of Lance's lifeline and continued to pull it apart from the twisted cable of the other three. I heard shouts coming from the kitchen, but didn't dare stop. Finally, I managed to disentangle Lance's soul from the others.

Shango's head lolled to one side. I don't think he was conscious anymore. Carefully, I lifted Lance's soul thread from among the twisted cords. There was a weakened section where Jinxey had been connected, which remained torn.

I carried the soul to Lance's inert body. I'd never given someone back their soul before; I had no idea what to do. His fading aura seemed to reach for it, like a mother for a long-lost child. Immediately, Lance's lifeline began to glow.

Lance stirred and gave me a confused look.

"How do you feel," I asked.

"Better." He cradled Jinxey in one hand while he flexed the other. "What did you do?"

Rhys came running out of the kitchen coughing, a billow of black smoke behind him. "We've got to get out of here. Someone's set the place on fire. The main stairs are already engulfed." He pointed to the stairs leading up to the entrance of Club Lapis. That's our only way out."

A gunshot rang out from the kitchen.

"Who's that?"

"Savanne." Rhys got Lance to his feet. He was alert, but still weak. I unfastened the straps binding Shango to the chair. He was too feeble to walk on his own.

The door to the kitchen banged open, and Savanne stumbled into the room, a gun in one hand, pointed at the three of us. She moved stiffly, as thick black smoke poured out of the kitchen behind her. Without Louis to animate her, she looked like a walking corpse.

"Leave him. He's mine!" She raised the pistol.

She was dying; that much was clear.

"No wait!" I held out the ankh. "I can give you back your soul, if we get him out of here." A fit of coughing came over me.

She shook her head. "I can't go back. You don't know what I've done. I loved him and he took everything. I'm already dead."

She was right. Her skin was a nightmare; a cloudy

film covered her eyes. By all rights, she shouldn't have been walking around. The smoke was so thick, I could barely breathe.

"Leave him. Like his son, he dies with me. Leave now or you will join him."

Shango's magic had been the only thing that had kept her moving this long. She was one of Morta's now. And that meant she answered to me.

"I command you, Savanne, put the gun--."

She pulled the trigger, and Shango's head snapped back. Rhys and I both jumped, and Shango tumbled lifelessly to the floor. She moaned and reached for him.

The last sight I had of Savanne and Shango were the two of them in a crumpled heap, as flames raced across the carpet toward them. With Rhys on one side and me on the other, we hauled Lance up the stairs into the fresh air and the sound of approaching fire trucks.

CHAPTER 37

A WEEK LATER, Rhys and I lay amid the tangled sheets of my lovely green room at the top of the stairs at Henri's place. The morning sun streamed in through the voile curtains, and outside the birds sang loud enough to wake the dead.

The authorities questioned all of us, but made no arrests. The upper part of the house on Bayshore was already in flames by the time we got out, and the fire department couldn't do much more than keep it from spreading to the neighboring homes. It wasn't until after the fire was out and the wreckage gone through by the arson investigators that we were finally off the hook.

The gun was found with Savanne and Shango. Police investigators said it was used to kill both Shango and his son, Evan. Mimsy's body was found in a shallow grave in the sub-basement, along with two others, as yet unidentified. Manner of death not yet determined, but Lance, Chen, Rhys, and I were all exonerated. The press called it a bizarre voodoo cult.

Rhys snuggled closer, wrapping his naked body around mine.

I sighed with contentment. Rhys told me he'd been worried I was only attracted to him because of Morta's legacy, just as I thought he was attracted only to me because I was the Hand of Fate.

It didn't matter.

Chen left yesterday. Rhys and I drove him to the airport for his two-day flight back to Shanghai. He was in amazingly good spirits for a guy who lost the woman he was supposed to marry and came pretty damn close to losing his soul and his life as well. I don't think he'll be making plans to come back any time soon.

Lance went into rehab the day after the police finished questioning him. He's in a residential treatment program in Syracuse; the best in the state. For the next month at least, he'll be safe and getting the help he needs.

Rhys spoke into my neck. "What did you decide?"

While the idea of moving in with Rhys sounded appealing, I wasn't ready yet. I liked waking up to the sounds of birds and the smell of sweet mown grass. His apartment above Mystic Properties was noisy with street traffic in the morning, and there was a loud and rowdy bar right next door. Besides, I'd promised to teach Henri how to drive, and he loves doing housework and laundry, which works great for me. He's the perfect roommate.

For driving practice, I let Henri drive Rusty and me to Heavenly Shores Amusement Park. There were a couple more things I needed to do before I put this mess behind me and focused on my new future as the Hand of Fate.

Yeah, that's me. Now that I've accepted it, I'm trying to work on owning it.

I left Henri in the car, and took the winding path leading down to the beach. Luhng was just rising to the surface as I reached the narrow sand at the lakeshore. Larry, my little lizard, no, *djragon djemon* porpoised through the water ahead of Luhng, and wag-tailed himself up the shore to me, a big grin on his reptilian face. He immediately flopped over onto his back so I could rub his cold, wet belly.

"I sure missed you, little one." I tickled him, and he squeaked delightedly; his toes curling with obvious pleasure. I called to Blix, and left my two *djemons* to entertain each other. Blix was now noticeably bigger than Larry.

Luhng emerged from the water more sedately, and with far less enthusiasm. His energy hit me with the same force I'd felt in our earlier encounters, but today he fairly bristled with resentment.

I nodded my head to him politely, but would not bow or allow him to intimidate me. Mimsy was dead; both of us had played a role in that.

I held out the wooden box which held the clay pipe, left behind by Mimsy on our last visit here together. "I am returning this, that you may remember happier times with Miriam."

The density of the air around us abated, although his scowl remained unchanged.

"The husband her mother and I chose for her was a good son of the *djragon*. She would have grown to love him. Instead she defied me."

I nodded. "I met him. Chen is a fine man, but I think Mimsy wanted to choose her own destiny."

"Of course you would say that. You know nothing of tradition. Of responsibility. Of legacy."

I sighed. Nothing I could say would sway Luhng's millenniums-old beliefs. "That brings me to Larry."

A swift expression of anguish crossed his face, and the pressure built up around us to an uncomfortable level. In that instant, I knew I was making the right decision, and in spite of my feelings for Larry, I had to do what was best for him.

With the exception of Savanne's *djemon*, Sorroh, none of Shango's *djemons* had any skills which would have allowed them to function in society. Their masters had treated them like beasts, and so they remained. Louis and the others would have become extremely dangerous to humans once Shango died. Of the eight or so very large *djemons* I'd encountered since becoming the Hand of Fate, only three, Oneiri, Sorroh, and Luhng had any sort of education and formal training. As I was determined to educate Blix, I wanted to be sure that Larry would also benefit from the best education available.

"I was hoping that you would agree to continue to tutor Larry for me."

His furrowed brow smoothed, and the oppressive air around us abated somewhat. "In my care, he cannot grow. When you, his master dies, he will perish in the transformation and all his education will have been wasted."

"If I instruct him to obey you as my proxy, I believe he will grow. As his instructor, you would have him study, practice, and learn continuously. He has already grown somewhat since I saw him last, so even though he's smaller than Blix, I know it will work. I can come back to check on his progress in a few months. I think this is the best solution for Larry, if you are willing, Luhng."

As if on cue, Larry turned away from Blix, and scampered back to Luhng. Without hesitation, he clambered up the *djragon's* scaly leg and up to his shoulder, where he perched as if this were his accustomed spot.

Luhng gave me a slight nod. "You surprise me, child of Morta. So be it."

I found Charlie Crimmer at the Midway, watching over a gang of boisterous kids at the Shoot-the-Zombie game.

He greeted me with a grin and a hug that took me by surprise. His uniform was clean and neatly pressed. His iron-grey hair neatly braided in a long tail down his back, and his eyes twinkled with good humor. Even his shoes were shined.

I scarcely recognized him.

"I'm glad you're here. Come on, I've got something to show ya." He set off at a brisk pace, nothing like the doddering, cranky old man I remembered.

We headed toward the Shriek Shanty. "I wanted to thank ya. I mean for Annie and all. I think I'm healed, Er, my soul at any rate. I'm feelin' a lot better."

As we reached the sub-basement, Annie appeared on his shoulder. He gave her an affectionate pat. "I keep her down here, so's nobody can see her. As you can see, she's feelin' better, too."

He paused at the bottom of the stairs to give me a better look. The little pterodactyl's wings were completely healed. More than that, she looked far less fragile than I'd ever seen her. I'd had my doubts that transferring her to Charlie would work, but there was no doubt that it had.

"She looks great."

"And look at this," he motioned me over to the open portal.

When I peeked over the edge, not a soul rose to greet me.

"Where are they?"

"That's what I'm tryin' to tell you. They're not afraid of me no more. I got my soul back." He pounded his chest. "I'm whole again."

"I believe you are. Glad to see it, Charlie." Rhys told me his soul would have eventually healed anyway, but seeing Charlie and Annie both looking so well made me feel great.

"I hate to ask, but if you like, I can banish her for you." I held my hand up. "No, not like last time, I can to do it properly now. It won't hurt either of you."

Charlie pursed his lips into a thin line for a moment, then shook his head. "I don't think so. I learnt me a real lesson with Snot-wad, and I like to think I'm a man as kin still learn lessons, even at my age. Annie and me are just fine as we are. She's good comp'ny. An' smart. I read to her at night, and she's already figgered out some of the words. Who'da thought a little thing like her would be needin' an old codger like me? I guess I'm just tryin' to say we're just fine like we are, thanks anyways."

CHAPTER 38

I PULLED INTO the driveway, just as Henri and Rhys were re-hanging the freshly painted Hand of Fate sign from the roof of the front porch. The big yellow, fortuneteller sign looked even bigger with the new paint job. And seeing my name spelled out in big, blood-red letters; well, in spite of myself, I winced.

HAND OF FATE
MATTIE BLACKMAN
BY APPOINTMENT ONLY

Both men had sweated through their tee-shirts in the heat. Wrestling that heavy thing back onto the chains which had held it for half a century hadn't been easy.

"We wanted to surprise you," Henri said. "Don't you like it?"

They both looked so proud of themselves.

"It's big, isn't it?" A bold statement, that. Not something the casual observer would miss. "Is it just me, or is it bigger?"

Rhys handed me an envelope. "Got something for you."

My pulse quickened.

"Yeah," Henri added. "A lady from Mayor Brunson's office dropped it by. It's the formal invitation to be the Grand Marshal of this year's Spirit Festival. Madame did it every year. This year marks their fiftieth anniversary."

I opened the envelope and scanned the letter.

Hells bells. People from all over the world would descend on Shore Haven and I'd be right smack in the middle of the whole tamale. *Guest of Honor,* belle of the ball, queen of the chaos. My picture front and center on every poster. No more Mattie the meter maid. My life as a private citizen was officially over. A little scary.

They must've seen something on my face.

"What?" Henri looked as if he was about to cry. I realized he'd probably been looking forward to attending the festival. Rhys too. "You *have* to do it!"

Rhys gave me a smirk. "No, of course you don't have to do it." He sighed. "Come on, Henri. Help me take the sign down."

"No, I'm in! I'll do it." I grinned.

Okay, maybe I was gritting my teeth, just a little.

"And leave the sign. I like it just the way it is."

END

ABOUT THE AUTHOR

Award-winning author Sharon Joss writes science fiction, fantasy and horror. She is the author of six novels, including the AURUM, BROTHERS OF THE FANG, and the alternate history thriller, STEAM DOGS.

In 2015 , she won the Writers of the Future Golden Pen award for speculative fiction with her novella, *Stars That Make Dark Heaven Light.*

She lives amid a thicket of blackberry vines in Oregon and writes full-time.

If you want to be notified when Sharon Joss's next novel or collection is released, please sign up for the mailing list by going to *http://www.sharonjoss.com* Your email address will never be shared and you can unsubscribe at any time

Word of mouth and reviews are vital for any author to succeed. If you enjoyed the book, please tell your friends and consider leaving a review wherever you purchased it.

If you enjoyed
LEGACY SOUL,
be sure not to miss
the further adventures of Mattie and her friends in

CHAOS KARMA